The Big Swim of the Summer

By the same author

Trebizon School series

First Term at Trebizon
Second Term at Trebizon
Summer Term at Trebizon
Boy Trouble at Trebizon
More Trouble at Trebizon
The Tennis Term at Trebizon
Summer Camp at Trebizon
Into the Fourth at Trebizon
The Hockey Term at Trebizon

Me, Jill Robinson and the television quiz
Me, Jill Robinson and the seaside mystery
Me, Jill Robinson and the Christmas pantomime
Me, Jill Robinson and the school camp adventure

A Horse Called September
The Quicksilver Horse

ANNE DIGBY

The Big Swim of the Summer

DRAGON
Granada Publishing

Dragon Books
Granada Publishing Ltd
8 Grafton Street, London W1X 3LA

Published by Dragon Books 1979
Reprinted 1985

A Dragon Original

ISBN 0-583-30294-7

Printed and bound in Great Britain by
Anchor Brendon Ltd, Tiptree, Essex

Set in Intertype Times

Contents

CHAPTER ONE

A Good Swim

The very first time that Sara set eyes on Evelyn, it was a hot day in June. She saw her coming out of the telephone box at the top of Hocking Hill. Her curiosity was aroused from the very first moment.

Sara Townsend and Davy Smith had just toiled up to the top of the hill on their bikes. The sun was so hot that Sara's shirt was sticking to her back and Davy's new trousers were rolled up right above his knees. They were on their way to the swimming baths.

'Bet there's a queue,' grumbled Davy, his legs aching from having to stand on the pedals for the last bit of the hill.

'It was all right yesterday,' said Sara.

'Wasn't hot yesterday.'

'Well, I promised Tommy, didn't I?' said Sara, slightly on the defensive. 'To swim every day, right through half-term.'

'Oh, I don't mind queueing,' laughed Davy. 'It's going to be so fantastic just getting wet today.'

'Getting wet, and that's about all.'

'Yes, it'll be packed. You won't get much done, will you, Titch?'

'What difference does it make anyway?' sighed Sara. 'Everyone knows Kate Munro's going to win again this year.'

'Rubbish.'

'Tommy's a marvellous coach but she can't perform miracles.'

'She thinks she can. She's not doing too badly with you, or the others, come to that.'

Anita Thomas was the new PE teacher at Hocking School and had a special interest in swimming. She had been an English Junior swimmer herself and she had decided to enter a girl from the school for the Jane Cup. That was the real class event of the summer in this part of the country. Several girls who had won it in previous years had gone on to make a name for themselves as swimmers.

She hoped to find a girl not only good enough to enter, but good enough to win. Hocking was a fairly new school and she wanted to put it on the map. The girls liked Tommy's idea because there were some very good swimmers amongst them. Even the boys were taking an interest. But the trouble was that the real competition was right here in the same town; under their noses. Kate Munro went to the other school in Hocking, Ladymount, and the previous year had been the youngest girl ever to win the Jane Cup at Bardsley.

'Well, no miracles today,' said Sara. 'I'm so hot I could die. I just want to get into that water.'

They coasted along the top of the hill. They braked and dismounted by the telephone box at the entrance to the park. If they wheeled their bikes, they could take the short cut through the park to the swimming baths.

Ahead of them, the girl came out of the phone box.

Her shadow fell across their path and Sara looked up, startled.

She was an odd-looking girl, towering high above Sara. She was very tall and skinny and behind her spectacles she was crying. She walked with a round-shouldered slouch, as though ashamed of her height. Completely unaware of them she mooched in through the park gates, her feet scuffling into the gravel.

Sara had never noticed her around Hocking before.

'Let's go round by the trees, it's cooler,' said Davy.

They wheeled their bikes along the narrow path that led down through a grassy glade, shaded by cedar trees. Once out in the sunshine again, the light hurt their eyes for a moment. Flowers grew in profusion here and the mingled scents in the still, hot summer air were beautiful and subtle.

They came upon the girl again.

'Look!' said Sara in a whisper, touching Davy's arm.

She was kneeling on the grass now, by a flower bed. She had picked a rose and was savagely pulling it to pieces, scattering the petals all around her.

The girl heard them coming and leapt to her feet. For a moment she stared at them, as though in a daze, and then she blushed. Her eyes watering and rimmed with red, she turned and ran to the trees.

'She's gone,' said Davy. 'What an oddball. Was she the one who was in the phone box just now?'

'Yes,' said Sara.

She stared in silence at the mutilated flower lying on the grass.

'Oh heck,' groaned Davy. 'Just look at that queue.'

They had walked on now and could see the high walls of the Swimming Baths on the far side of the park. Outside the green iron turnstiles a queue of people clutching towels stretched far along the wall and round the corner out of sight.

They parked their bikes and took their places hopefully at the very end of the queue, their rolled towels under their arms. The white walls seemed to magnify the heat of the sun and they were sweltering now.

Inside they could hear the noise of people shouting and laughing and the cool sound of splashing water. Slowly the queue started to move. Sara revived as they came round the corner and within sight of the green turnstiles again.

'At least they're letting people in now,' she said.

But then, when they were fifty yards from the entrance, the queue stopped dead in its tracks. An attendant appeared.

'Sorry, full up,' he stated. 'No more admissions until six o'clock.'

Sara could have screamed.

'Never mind, we'll come back after tea,' said Davy taking her arm.

'I can't. I'm baby-sitting.'

They decided to take a short cut home, down the bridle path through Spindle Woods which lay on the other side of Hocking Hill.

They were out of the sun now but, deprived of her swim, Sara felt sticky all over and the heat was more than she could bear. She hadn't even the strength to talk to Davy as their bikes bumped down over the rough track. They passed a woman riding, and even the horse looked parched as it walked up the slope, its breathing laboured, its tail swishing away the flies. Later they learnt that it had been the hottest June day for years.

They saw the lake, and it was like a mirage. Through the gap in the trees they could see the cool grey water glistening in the sunlight, tantalizing them. It was the Munros' private lake, of course, at the far corner of the big grounds of Spindle House where Kate Munro and her family lived. There was an acre of woodland between the lake and the big house.

They laid down their bikes, took their swimming things and crept through the shrubs to the wooden palings that marked the boundary of the Munros' property. There were gaps in the fence. The lake was very close now, silent and deserted. There were two timber changing huts, a wooden diving board and a white punt moored by the shore. Some ducks were swimming.

'Shall we?' whispered Sara, excited and nervous.

They had seen the lake often enough before, but the thought had never entered their heads. Today the sun was affecting them. The temptation was quite irresistible.

'Let's,' said Davy, in no doubt about it.

They squeezed through the palings, scampered across to the huts and changed into their swimming things. Sara ran out along the diving board, jack-knifed into the water and surfaced ten yards out from shore laughing in exhilaration.

'Come on, Davy. It's fantastic.'

He joined her in the water. They were cool, at last.

Sara broke into a strong crawl, heading across the lake. Her arms moved almost lazily, but her feet paddling up and down in a swift rhythm left a wake of frothing water, marking her passage. She was soon leaving Davy far behind.

'Great, Sara. You're getting better all the time.'

He trod water for a while, enjoying the sun and watching her effortless strokes with admiration. If only she could win the Jane Cup this year – the big swim! Of course, the odds were hardly even when Kate Munro had this huge lake all to herself, and a father who could pay for a private swimming coach.

'Grrrr!'

Two figures emerged from the wood that lay between the lake and Spindle House. It was Kate Munro and her father, and they had a large Alsatian dog with them.

'Sara!' yelled Davy in alarm.

Out in the middle of the lake, Sara blinked the water out of her eyes, gulped in air, and saw them. She turned and started to swim strongly for the shore. She caught up with Davy by the changing huts, and her heart was beating very fast. What were they doing here? Why had they been so silly?

'After them, Prince!' Kate Munro cried in a shrill voice.

Sara rushed into the hut and scooped up her clothes. As Davy emerged from the hut next door the Alsatian leapt up at him and snapped his trousers out of his hands.

'Grrrrr!' The dog raced off with Davy's best lightweight trousers and took them to his mistress's feet. Savagely he started to paw them, ripping at the material with his teeth.

'Hey – stop him!' yelled Davy. 'They're my best pants!'

'They *were*, you mean!' laughed the red-haired girl.

Sara stared at Kate Munro in astonishment. The petulant anger had gone. She was enjoying herself immensely, egging the dog on.

'Tear them to pieces!' she continued. It was giving her pleasure, the sound of the material ripping.

'My pants!' Furiously Davy lunged forward towards the dog. But Mr Munro got there first and seized the Alsatian by the scruff of the neck.

'Drop 'em, Prince.'

With an expressionless face, the man handed Davy his ruined trousers.

'Let that be a lesson to you, lad. Now – get off my land.'

When they got back to their bikes, Davy spread his trousers out on the ground and spoke for the first time.

'Mum will kill me for this,' he said hoarsely.

'And *I* could kill Kate Munro,' said Sara, white-faced. 'There was no need for that.'

When she said good-bye to Davy at his house, which was just a few doors along from hers, she silently swore revenge.

CHAPTER TWO

The Unfriendly New Girl

The weather broke the next day and it was cloudy when Sara got to school.

'Don't worry, we'll have our session, short of a downpour,' said Tommy with a smile, when she saw her by the cycle sheds. 'We've got to get your racing start right, it's still too slow.'

Sara smiled back. She was looking forward to her training session with a new determination. If only she could be single-minded enough, perhaps anything was possible.

When she got to the classroom she found that a new desk had been placed between hers and Terry Horn's. Terry had long straight hair and believed he was irresistible to girls. He nudged the new desk with a proprietary air.

'New bird coming. Sitting next to me – my luck, eh? She's Legg, E.'

'She's leggy?' asked Sara. It was unusual for someone to start at half-term. 'Have you seen her then? What's she like?'

'No – that's her name. Legg, E. It's on the list.'

There was a sudden hush as someone came in. Sara was sorting out her books and the first thing she noticed was Terry's face. It sagged with disappointment. Then she heard someone say: 'Are you the new girl? That's your desk over there.'

Sara glanced up and caught her breath.

The girl was even taller than she remembered and as

skinny as a rake. She still walked with her shoulders hunched, and her eyes were glittering behind her spectacles as if she found the whole world hateful.

It was the girl who had been in the park. What a horrible shock! She shrank back as the new girl brushed against her to get to her desk.

Then their eyes met. As the girl recognized Sara from the park, a dull red flush crept up her cheeks and she quickly raised the lid of her desk and buried herself behind it. She took exercise books and a pencil case out of her satchel and carefully, methodically, laid them out inside.

Sara rose to her feet to go to Assembly. Terry Horn had been looking forward to proving how irresistible he was, but not any more. He was over by the window with a group of other boys and they were glancing across, snorting with laughter.

'Her name's Legg, E. Leggy – get it?'

'It fits. Never saw such a lanky shanks.'

'Well have to do something about her desk, eh?'

Outside the hall, after Assembly, Sara saw Davy, who was in a class above her. In the hall he, too, had recognized Leggy from the previous day.

'Fantastic.'

'She's in for a tough time, I think,' said Sara. Over the first shock, she could smile about it now. 'Terry Horn and friends have definitely got something up their sleeves.'

'Serves her right for looking so unfriendly,' said Davy. 'Honestly, she was looking around Assembly as though someone had just let a stink bomb off right under her nose.'

'There's something eating her all right.' Then Sara changed the subject. 'How did you get on about the trousers?'

'Mum was livid,' stated Davy. It made him angry to think about it. 'The dog made a real dinner of them. They can't even be repaired.'

'Spoilt, isn't she?' said Sara scornfully. 'I hate her. But we'll get our own back.'

'How?' asked Davy.

'Just an idea,' said Sara mysteriously. ' 'Bye, Davy – we'd better rush.'

Everyone else had gone to their classrooms. Sara and Davy went their separate ways. As she walked along the corridor, she dreamed a dream – of snatching the Jane Cup from under Kate Munro's nose this year. She imagined the cheers as she touched home to victory, the grateful look on Davy's face. If she worked at her swimming as she had never worked before, perhaps she could do it. It would be great to see that red-haired wonder from Ladymount School taken down a peg or two.

'Hurry up, Sara,' said Mr Arkwright, as she came in to class.

Everyone was sitting down at their desks. As Sara came up the gangway to take her place she glanced at the new girl's desk. There was something distinctly odd about it. It was towering above all the others, only in a lop-sided kind of way.

'I hope that you have all returned refreshed from your half-term holiday,' Old Noah was saying. As well as being their form master he taught them English, first period, every day. 'Now we shall all get down to brass tacks, or should I say, syntax.'

There was laughter from Tracey Smart in the front row, who always made a point of appreciating Old Noah's little jokes. But Leggy was rattling her desk ferociously, trying to straighten it out.

Sara's eyes strayed down to the floor, and then she stuffed a fist into her mouth to muffle her laughter. Under each of the four legs of Leggy's desk there was an assorted pile of textbooks, pencil boxes and shoe bags, magnificently elevating the desk.

'What's the matter with it?' the new girl muttered under her breath. 'Why's it so high up—?'

'Leg-room for Leggy!' mouthed Terry Horn across to Sara. He and some of the other boys were wide-eyed with suppressed delight.

As the tall girl tried to kick away the objects from under the legs of the desk, it started to sway dangerously.

'Look out!' Sara blurted out.

Her warning came too late. The desk crashed over into the new girl's lap. It made a terrible noise and the boys guffawed.

A large bottle of red drawing ink, open on top of the desk, spurted into Leggy's face and all over her blouse. She sprang up with a scream. The desk crashed right over, landing on her toes, and the red ink splattered down her socks.

'Aaagh!'

For a few seconds there was pandemonium as people rushed from their desks, crowding round, picking things up, maximizing the drama of the incident.

Leggy just stood there. Her ferociousness had gone. She looked rather forlorn and bewildered, red ink dripping down her face, a great smudge of it under her nose. Old Noah came over and glowered.

'Will those responsible for this come and see me after the lesson,' he said crisply. He looked furious. Then he glanced at Sara. 'Take Evelyn to the cloakroom,' he said.

They walked side by side down the corridor, in embarrassed silence. Sara went and got her games shirt.

'You'd better change into this,' she said, as the new girl found a wash-basin and started to unbutton her blouse.

For the first time the girl saw her face in the mirror. She stared.

Then suddenly she made a sound.

It was just a low gurgle at first, and Sara wasn't sure whether she was laughing or crying. Then her shoulders started to heave.

'Oh ... oh ... oh!' Tears of laughter were streaming down her cheeks. 'Oh!' It was so infectious that Sara started to giggle too.

'I look like a prize fighter!' shrieked Leggy. 'Look at my bloody nose!'

They giggled and giggled; they even clung to each other for a moment, weak-kneed. Sara hadn't enjoyed herself so much for ages.

At last the laughter subsided and Leggy got down to the serious business of washing and changing. But for a while, at least, the cold angry look had left her face and the warm flush that lingered on her cheeks made her distinctly attractive.

Sara felt relieved. The girl was human, after all! Perhaps it wasn't going to be so bad, having to sit next to her in class.

'Your name's Evelyn, then?'

'That's right. Evelyn Legg.'

'I'm afraid you've got a nickname already – Leggy. Do you mind if I call you that?'

'Call me what you like, Sara.' The girl shrugged. 'It doesn't make any difference to me.'

After that she shut up like a clam.

CHAPTER THREE

Sara's Promise

The last lesson of the afternoon was Geography. Sara found it extremely difficult to concentrate on the Nile Delta. She kept gazing out of the window. There was heavy, threatening cloud in the sky, and if there should be a downpour then her special coaching session with Tommy would have to be postponed. But about five minutes before the bell went, the sun burst through a gap in the clouds for the first time that day, as if in answer to a prayer.

Sara collected up her swimming things and ran out of the school building, over to the swimming pool. The sun was dancing on the blue water, making it sparkle, and, full of anticipation, she sang to herself as she changed in one of the cubicles.

'Hello.'

Tommy was waiting at the side of the pool, at the deep end.

She was not only tanned, and fit, and glamorous; she was also an extremely nice person and thus was liked by girls and boys alike at the school. At the moment her light blue swimming suit made her body look very brown and supple. She was, as always, punctual to the second.

'Hello, Tommy.'

'Let's work on that start of yours, Sara. Come and stand here.'

The coaching session would last only fifteen minutes, and after that it would be someone else's turn. Tommy chose to give the most promising swimmers individual tuition. Sara intended to make the most of her session today.

'Now, swing your arms at your side, loosen up. Right. Now, legs absolutely straight as you hit the water – arms stretched above your head as far as they will go. Fingers leading, thumbs together, palms down.'

Sara dived and surfaced.

'No, you were slightly bent at the knees and elbows and your glide was too long – try again.'

There were several onlookers sitting round the pool as Sara took up her starting position again. She noted that both Hilda Matthews and Jane Thomas were there, watching and listening. She was slightly faster than both of them, but there wasn't much in it.

Sara did four dives and then Tommy took over – clearly demonstrating where she had gone wrong.

On the sixth dive Sara got it right – skimming into the water as straight as a flat stone, a short glide just two feet under the surface and then coming up fast with one arm pull and feet paddling, ready to move at speed.

'That's more like it.' It was good to see the approving smile on Tommy's face as she clambered out. 'Didn't it feel better?'

'Yes, it felt absolutely right.'

'Now take a short rest and then I'll time you over 100 metres. You'll clip up to a second off your time if you can start like that.'

As Sara came forward, after a rest, to swim four lengths, she noticed someone else had joined the onlookers. It was Leggy. She was sitting on a wooden bench, far apart from all the others, looking towards the pool with a cold and supercilious expression. Sara was amazed to see her, and thought:

'She's got her "stink-bomb" look again. I'll show her!'

She made a perfect racing start and did four lengths of the swimming pool in a powerful crawl, head down, body cleaving through the water. Even before Tommy showed her the stop-watch, she felt exhilarated.

'You've clipped one-and-a-half seconds off your previous best. Well done.'

Sara was tired now and put a towel round her shoulders. Tommy smiled.

'You really made an effort today.'

'I've decided I'd like to win the big swim,' said Sara, surprised at her own outspokenness. 'I wouldn't like to see Kate Munro win it two years running.'

'We'll have to see what Hilda and Jane have to say about that,' said Tommy, delighted. Only one girl could go through to Bardsley, and the PE teacher enjoyed pitting them against each other. 'All the same, you've done well today.'

Sara got dressed and came out of the cubicle, glowing.

Tommy was talking to Leggy and her voice was raised.

'Nonsense, my dear. If you can't swim, the sooner you learn the better.'

'I have no intention of taking part in swimming,' said the tall girl, angry and scornful. 'It's not compulsory, surely?'

'It most certainly is. There's a swimming lesson tomorrow. You be there.'

Tommy walked away.

Having lost the argument, Leggy seemed to crumple up.

'She's crying,' thought Sara, shocked. 'She looks quite different.'

The eyes that usually glittered disdainfully behind the glasses, as though the world were a dreadful place, now glistened with forlorn tears. Once again, her hauteur had vanished.

Tommy was aware of none of this. Brisk and confident in her Cambridge blue swim-suit, she was now talking to Hilda Matthews up at the other end of the pool.

'Why doesn't Leggy want to learn to swim?' wondered Sara. 'Oh, dear. She does look miserable.'

Sara decided that Evelyn Legg's hauteur was something of an act. At the moment she looked lonely and scared of people – especially confident, glamorous people like Anita Thomas. Not for the first time, Sara sensed a mystery.

'I'm sure she *has* got something on her mind. But what?'

The tall girl started to drift away from the pool, like a sleepwalker.

'Leggy – please wait!' Sara called out. On impulse, she ran until she caught up with her, and then she slipped an arm round her waist. 'What's the matter?'

'Sara!' The other girl looked startled. 'I didn't see you.'

'I was getting changed. I heard your row with Tommy.'

'I hate her. She can't make me swim – she can't.'

'She can.'

When they entered the cycle shed the sun came out from behind a cloud and a shaft of light beamed in through the open door, making the metal cycle racks dazzling and bright in the dusky shed. It was as though this were too much for Leggy. She flung herself against the wall, with her back to Sara, and heaved with noisy sobs.

'I don't want to join in swimming lessons – I don't want to join in anything. I feel – I feel like burying myself in a hole.'

'Shut up, please don't cry.' Sara pulled the girl round to face her. For the second time that afternoon her own words surprised her: 'You need a friend, don't you? What on earth have you got against swimming?'

Leggy blinked at Sara through her tears, surprised and touched.

'I – I–'

'I say, you're not scared of water, are you?'

Leggy seized on Sara's words eagerly.

'Yes, that's it.' She buried her face in her hands. 'I'm petrified – always have been and always will be. But Tommy wouldn't understand. Not that – that Amazon.'

'No, she wouldn't,' agreed Sara. 'But I do. My cousin's terrified of water, too. Gosh, you poor thing. Now I understand.'

Leggy pushed up her spectacles and wiped her eyes and they both collected their bikes. Sara's mind was busy. She must think of some way, any way, of putting Leggy out of her misery.

'I'll help you,' she said, at last.

'How?' Leggy's expression was hopeful.

'I'm good at doing grown-up handwriting,' Sara admitted in a rush, not sure what had come over her. 'Have you any objections?'

'None,' said Leggy. 'None whatsoever.'

They wheeled their bikes towards the school gates, whispering together.

'Can you get to school early tomorrow? Meet me at the cycle sheds? Bring something in your mother's handwriting, and some of her stationery.'

'You bet.'

Leggy's tear-stained radiance was ample reward for Sara. It was marvellous to have made someone so happy. She cycled home to tea, feeling like a fairy godmother.

In bed that night she was seized with panic at what she had promised to do. Working a fiddle! Forging a note!

The boys did it sometimes, but not her – not Sara Townsend!

It was ages before she could sleep.

'I don't know how it's come about,' she thought in despair, 'but Leggy and I are going to be friends. I can't let her down now – I can't break my promise.'

CHAPTER FOUR

Advice from an Odd Quarter

'Why aren't you in your swimming things, Evelyn?' asked Tommy the next day, the light of battle in her eyes.

Sara, standing at the side of the pool in her swim-suit, glanced across at Leggy and held her breath. The tall girl handed the PE teacher an envelope, her face expressionless.

'I've brought a note from my mother, Miss Thomas.'

The teacher ripped open the envelope and read the note; she seemed to colour slightly under her tan.

'You can't take part in swimming or games – for medical reasons. I see. You might have explained that yesterday, Evelyn, instead of getting involved in a foolish argument with me.' She nodded. 'Very well – fetch a school textbook. You may sit out here and do some reading; you might as well get some fresh air while you're about it.'

'Thank you, Miss Thomas.'

During this exchange, Sara had barely dared to listen, Her hands had gone clammy and she could feel the goose pimples coming out on her arms.

Now she felt quite faint with relief. Leggy passed very close to her.

'Thanks,' she whispered, her eyes twinkling behind her big lenses. Sara turned away to hide a smile. She had succeeded – she had saved Leggy from the ordeal of swimming lessons! But back in the depths of her mind was a feeling of guilt, at the enormity of what she had done.

'Sara!'

She almost jumped out of her skin at the sound of Tommy's voice, and hurried over to her. But there was nothing to fear.

'Hilda! Jane! Come here please.'

'Yes?' asked Sara, as the three of them joined the teacher.

'I'm concentrating on the breast-stroke today. But you three can stay up this end and work on your crawl. I'll try and give you a few minutes later on. Okay?'

Sara nodded. She knew that she was in Tommy's good books after the successful coaching session yesterday, but she couldn't meet those friendly blue eyes. How awful it was to have a guilty conscience! Would she ever feel easy with the PE teacher again?

'Come on, you two, let's take it in turn to time each other,' suggested Hilda Matthews.

They were the three best Junior swimmers in the school; their times proved it. It was taken for granted that one of them would win the Heat to be held at the school shortly. The winner would then go through to represent Hocking School in the Jane Cup Championship at Bardsley, always referred to as 'the big swim' in the local press.

They threw themselves into swimming practice. Sara was delighted with her racing start now. She did four widths in all. Although the first was slightly slower than Janes's, the next three were consistently faster than the other girls' efforts.

Once or twice Sara caught Leggy watching them, but most of the time the tall girl just sat with her book open on her lap, staring into space.

'Hilda – you're still trying to twist on the somersault when you turn. You *must* twist on the push-off.'

Tommy had finished giving instructions to the rest of

the class. Now she was able to give her three 'stars' a little time. But all too soon the school bell sounded in the distance. It was Dinner Break.

'How would the three of you like to have a session after school?' asked the teacher. 'I'd like to see you race together – flat out. That's the best practice there is.'

The girls giggled, nervous and excited. Tommy glanced up at the sky.

'Four o'clock then, girls – as long as the weather holds.'

Before she got dressed, Sara had a warm shower. She felt a pleasant ache in her shoulder muscles. Swimming really was the most marvellous thing. Poor Leggy – she simply didn't know what she was missing. As she towelled herself vigorously, she thought again about the Jane Cup.

She imagined herself bringing it home to Hocking School in glorious triumph! This was her favourite day-dream now.

She was so long getting dressed that when she emerged the swimming pool was quite deserted. She came through the gate – and there was Leggy waiting for her. 'Hello, Sara!'

'Hello, Leggy,' she replied, pleased and surprised.

They walked slowly towards the distant school buildings, forgetting it was almost dinner-time.

Neither of them said a word about the forged note. It was a secret bond between them now. Sara was surprised that she felt a kind of relaxed contentment in this odd girl's company. To think how she had been repelled by her on first sight!

Her mind went back to that strange encounter in the park, when Leggy had savagely mutilated a flower. Shortly before that she had been speaking to someone on the phone, in the public box at the top of the hill. Did she nurse some secret hate against the world? And if so – why?

'Sara – I was watching you swim just then,' the tall girl said suddenly, breaking the silence. Her tone was casual. 'If you could only keep your legs straight, you could really go some.'

'Keep my legs straight?'

Sara stared at her new friend in astonishment.

'Yes – after you've been going a while you start to bend at the knees. It slows you down no end.'

'What on earth do *you*—'

'—know about it?' Leggy finished Sara's sentence, as though prepared for it. 'Yes, it must seem strange. But you see my – my fear of water has me rather obsessed with it, in a funny way. I've made a great study of swimming.'

'You have?'

Sara was speechless. What an odd girl she was!

'If you want to win the big swim – and you do, don't you? – you'll have to stop bending your knees.' Leggy spoke in a matter-of-fact way. 'Give it a try.'

They were just aproaching the Dining Hall. Someone was waiting patiently outside.

'Davy!' exclaimed Sara, putting her hand to her cheek.

He always waited for her there – and today she had clean forgotten about him! He came forward but frowned at the sight of Leggy.

'Hi, Titch,' he said. 'Coming?'

'Excuse me,' said Leggy in a stiff voice. 'I must dash and put this book back before I have dinner.'

'We'll save you a place—' Sara started to say.

But Leggy was scuttling away.

'What on earth do you see in her, Titch?' asked Davy, when they sat down in the Hall.

'I like her, I've decided. All that stand-offishness, it's just an act. She's an interesting person underneath. I think we're going to be friends.'

'Really?' muttered Davy. He watched Leggy when she came into the Hall, late. She carefully avoided their gaze, and the place Sara had saved her, and sat elsewhere. 'It doesn't look as though she thinks the same.'

Sara stabbed a cluster of hard school peas on to her fork, and wished that Leggy would present her nice side to the world. She suddenly wanted everyone to like Leggy as much as she did.

'How's the swimming?' asked Davy.

Sara told him about her racing start, and the good times she had been doing. She mentioned the practice race arranged for after school.

'Good, I'll watch,' said Davy.

All afternoon Leggy's 'tip' gnawed at Sara's mind. Surely she shouldn't take it seriously! Or should she?

At home time Leggy did not refer to it. She said simply:

'Good luck with the practice race, Sara. And – thanks for what you did today, getting me out of swimming.'

She was collecting her blazer from the cloakroom.

'Why don't you come and watch?' asked Sara.

'No, I won't, thanks.' The tall girl shook her head, 'Got to get home – I'm expecting a phone call.'

She flung her blazer on quickly and hurried out of the cloakroom, hair untidy, all arms and legs – just as Terry Horn and his gang came round the corner. Terry stuck out his foot and Leggy went crashing across the corridor.

'Oops! Enjoy your trip?' sniggered Terry, as Leggy picked herself up.

Leggy just stared at him, her hatred of the world returning. She hurried on her way.

'You creep!' snapped Sara. 'Can't you leave her alone?'

'My, we're very protective all of a sudden,' said Terry. He looked at Sara's swimming things. 'Going over to the pool? Mind if I come and watch?'

'You come near the pool and I'll push you in,' said Sara.

She hurried out of the school buildings, across the field and through the gate. The pool looked cool and inviting in the afternoon sun. Hilda and Jane were already in the water. Sara felt happy as she saw a tall tousled figure sitting on one of the benches. Davy had come to watch – just as he said he would.

'Hi, Sara.'

'Hi, Davy.'

When Sara emerged from her cubicle, two or three minutes later, Tommy had arrived. She had her swim-suit and towel under her arm and was wearing faded blue denim shorts and a t-shirt, looking even more tanned and fit than usual.

'Davy!' she said with a smile. 'How nice that you're here. Hold this.'

She handed Davy her stop-watch and disappeared to change.

'What's going on?' asked Sara.

'I fancy she's going to race with you,' laughed Davy. 'You'd better get in the water and loosen up.'

Sara did a beautiful racing dive from the edge, skimming into the water as straight as a knife. She surfaced and did an easy length.

'Right, girls,' Tommy was standing at the far end, waiting now.

They swam up, and clambered out beside her.

'I feel like a swim,' she said briskly. 'I want the four of us to race together. We'll do four lengths – that's 100 metres of course. The same as the Jane. Davy's going to time us. I want you to remember all I've taught you – and I expect to see some personal records broken.'

Sara shivered with excitement. For Tommy to race with them was a rare honour! She was fast – very fast. As a girl she had broken the English record over this distance.

She was looking forward to the race.

CHAPTER FIVE

Davy Disapproves

While the girls rested, the PE teacher swam a length to limber up, showing that she meant business. Hilda looked slightly nervous, but Sara felt pleased. This should ginger up their times a bit!

Soon the four figures were poised at the edge of the pool, their heads down, arms outstretched, four curved backs in a row. Davy put the PE whistle to his lips gazing intently at the stop-watch.

Wheeeee-eeee!

With a piercing blast from the whistle, they were off.

Sara skimmed into the water and surfaced just ahead of Hilda and Jane, but behind Tommy. She set her eyes on the bottom of the pool and broke into a strong, steady crawl. One of the first lessons the PE teacher had taught her was bi-lateral breathing, taking breath first on the left, then on the right, so that she could always keep an eye on her opponents on either side.

Now, as she forged strongly through the water, Sara saw that the three girls were almost level – while Tommy, in the next lane to her, was slowly easing ahead.

At the first turn both Hilda and Tommy were ahead, but Sara was conserving her energy. On and on she ploughed, keeping up a steady rhythm, arm over arm, drawing in a deep steady breath once every one-and-a-half-stroke cycles.

After the third and final turn at the far end of the pool, Sara knew that she was comfortably ahead of both Hilda and Jane and felt a surge of confidence. She knew she had something in reserve. Now for the finishing straight.

Tommy was well ahead, and starting to accelerate. But suddenly that flash of blue surging through the water was an affront to Sara – no longer a teacher, but a rival.

'She thinks she's going to thrash me. I won't let her. *I won't.*'

Sara started to shorten and speed up her pulls, sprinting fast. But Tommy, almost imperceptibly, was still drawing ahead. Now the blood was pounding in Sara's temples; she felt angry and frustrated; she was in danger of losing her rhythm.

Then quite suddenly a cool, authoritative voice echoed in her brain. Leggy's words were coming back to her.

'If you could only keep your legs straight – you could really go some.'

Sara knew she had to obey that voice in her head. One ... two ... three ... four. Her legs, firm and straight, edged up and down rapidly in the water, while from the ankle her feet paddled six times, to each stroke cycle. It was agonizing, exhausting. So she must have been bending them after all! This was much more difficult.

Somehow she kept it up. Then, as though from far away, she heard Davy's excited shout.

'Atta girl, Sara!'

She was holding the gap steady and then, slowly, she began to narrow the space between herself and Tommy. With a surge of excitement Sara knew, even in her exhausted state, that she had never swum as fast as this before. The last half length whipped by in a flurry of churning water and her fingertips touched home only seconds behind Tommy.

'Get Sara's time!' shouted the teacher at that moment.

Hilda came in next, and Jane last, panting heavily. Sara leant against the side of the pool, face down on the cool tiles at the edge, getting her breath back. Then a friendly hand came down and gripped hers, and Tommy helped her out of the water. Davy had rushed up with the stop-watch.

'Sixty-six point four seconds, Titch!' he yelled, red in the face with excitement. 'Fantastic!'

Sara, still gulping for breath, could hardly believe it.

'Well done, Sara,' said Tommy quietly. There was no mistaking the pleasure in her voice. 'Sixty-six? That's good.'

She smiled encouragement at Hilda and Jane, who were treading water, looking a little forlorn.

'Well swum both of you.' She said 'And cheer up! Sara's the first one to go that fast – but you two are capable of the same thing. Remember it's ten days before we hold the Heat and decide who'll swim for the school.'

The other girls raised half-hearted smiles at that, but as the three of them went over to the changing cubicles, Tommy had eyes only for Sara.

Five minutes later, in warm dry clothes, she felt limp with satisfaction. It had been a good race.

'Come on, Titch. We're going to celebrate.'

While she had been changing, Davy had hurried over to the cycle sheds and collected their bikes. Now he took her by the arm.

'I'll buy you coffee down town. You need it.'

'Ouch!' said Sara, as they cycled out of the school gates. 'My legs are starting to ache.'

'I'm not surprised. I've never seen you swim like that before. Maybe you really can do it – get the Cup off Kate Munro this year.'

'Wouldn't that be just great?' said Sara.

As they cycled along they were both content to day-dream. Sara tried to imagine the look of fury and defeat on Kate's face as she overtook her on the final length. But the picture kept blurring.

They parked their bikes outside Take Two, the newest coffee bar in Hocking. Sara felt good then, sitting with Davy in the soft leather seats by the window, piped music playing above their heads.

'Mmm. Tastes luverly,' she said, as she sipped hot frothy coffee in a thick red pottery mug.

'I'll buy you a toasted sandwich, too,' said Davy. 'You must be starving.'

By the time she had eaten the sandwich, Sara felt marvellous. Now she and Davy could talk properly. She told him all about Leggy's surprising swimming 'tip' – and how it had come into her mind at the crucial moment.

'Good lord,' muttered Davy. 'Fancy that long-legged spider knowing anything about swimming. And her tip really worked!'

'Yes,' laughed Sara. 'And, Davy – I really do like her. In fact she's quite a kindred spirit. But she's certainly one of the oddest people I've ever met. Do you know she's made this great study of swimming in spite of the fact that she's terrified of water herself. In fact . . .'

In a rush of confidence, she told Davy how she had forged the note for Leggy to get her out of swimming. She felt goose-pimply again, just talking about it.

'You're crazy.' Davy looked annoyed. 'You must like her a lot to have done a thing like that. You'll be in it up to your neck if it ever comes out.'

'I know,' said Sara, suddenly feeling miserable. 'I don't know what came over me. It just seemed terribly important to get her off the hook.'

'Oh, cheer up.' He smiled and pretended to punch her lightly on the nose. 'It may never happen.'

She felt better.

At that moment the door shuddered open and a crowd of girls flocked in, all talking and laughing at once, shattering the quiet atmosphere that the friends had been enjoying. They were all wearing the pink-and-grey striped blazers of Ladymount School, which was on the same side of town as Take Two.

The slim, red-haired one was the centre of attention.

'Coffee all round!' she cried in a shrill voice.

'No, Kate,' said an earnest-looking girl. 'The idea is that we treat *you*.'

Davy and Sara went stiff. Here was Kate Munro herself, even more full of swagger than usual. As she came past their table she paused and stared at them, a sarcastic expression on her face.

'Enjoyed any good swimming lately?'

'Better than you think,' smiled Davy. 'But pardon us. We forgot that Take Two was one of your haunts. Come on, Sara.'

With studied dignity, they got to their feet and Davy paid the bill at the door.

As they came outside, the excited talk and laughter followed them, echoing in the narrow street.

'They seem to be celebrating something,' said Sara, frowning at her bike. 'I wonder what?'

'Who cares?' said Davy. 'They give me the creeps. They act as though they own the town sometimes. Let's go.'

As they cycled home together, they laughed and joked. Davy said good-bye to her at her garden gate.

Yet, as she wheeled her bike round to the shed at the back, Sara found her thoughts returning to Kate Munro and her friends. What on earth had they been celebrating? Their jubilation filled her with an obscure sense of foreboding.

CHAPTER SIX

The Newspaper Headline

'You look pleased with yourself this morning,' said Mrs Townsend.

'Mmmm?' Sara looked guilty. 'Do I?'

She had been munching her breakfast slowly and staring at the cornflakes packet with a silly smile on her face. Her obscure worry about Kate Munro had vanished this morning. Instead she had woken up with the realization that she, Sara Townsend, had swum 100 metres in under 67 seconds. She remembered the unmistakable pleasure on Tommy's face.

'I – I was looking at this competition,' lied Sara. 'A thousand transistor radios to be won! Imagine it.'

'And where would we put all those?' said her mother drily.

Somehow Sara couldn't confide her hopes about the big swim to her mother. Those hopes were too fragile and precious for parents' ears. Her time in the practice race had surprised everybody, even herself.

Evelyn Legg, however, was not surprised.

'I knew you could swim faster if you kept your legs straight,' she said flatly during morning break at school. She stared without expression at the glass of squash in her hand as she spoke. They were sitting on the wall outside the Dining Hall.

'You're a genius,' laughed Sara. 'You dark horse! Fancy your having read it all up. I didn't even believe you at first. But gosh, you were right, I start off with them straight and then begin to bend at the knees as I get tired—'

She stopped speaking. Leggy was still staring into her squash, as though there were an insect floating in it. She was very morose this morning.

'What's the matter?'

'Nothing.'

'There is, I can tell.' Sara touched the girl's arm. Although no one else liked her very much, not even Davy, she felt an increasing affinity with her. 'I didn't mean to laugh at you, not being able to swim.'

'Oh, it's not that.' Tears were welling into the tall girl's eyes; Sara's friendship had a softening effect on her. She swallowed her drink noisily, and then she stood up. 'It's just – well – I was expecting a phone call last night. And it didn't come.'

With that, Leggy walked away.

'Hey—' Sara stood up and then sat down again on the low wall.

Leggy had disappeared into the Dining Hall with her empty glass, completely switched off.

It suddenly occurred to Sara that she knew nothing about this girl who had just moved to Hocking. Where did she live exactly? What were her parents like? Had she any brothers or sisters? She never mentioned them – she never talked about herself at all.

'She's a complete mystery.' She shivered a little as a cloud passed in front of the morning sun, throwing the world in shadow for a minute. 'Why do I like her? I simply can't imagine!'

It was a relief to sit next to Davy at dinner-time. He was such a normal, happy-go-lucky person. They talked about his exams and then they talked a lot about swimming.

'I know Leggy gave you a good tip,' conceded Davy reluctantly. 'But I think what really helped was racing against Tommy – it was a real challenge for you. Let's face it, you outclass Hilda and Jane now. They're not fast enough to provide you with the stiff competition you need.'

'I – I don't know about that—' Sara shrugged. She attacked her lemon-curd tart with her spoon. It was as hard as iron today. 'But it certainly was terrific racing with Tommy. If only I could race against her all the time – have her as my own private coach!'

Davy laughed, and then shrugged. The girls' PE teacher at Hocking School was far too busy to give one girl more than a fraction of her time.

A wistful expression crossed Sara's face as she thought of her rival. Kate, apart from having so much talent, also had all the luck. Ladymount had a heated indoor pool where you could swim all the year round, and of course she had her own private lake at home, as well as Grundy – her very own swimming coach!

Thinking about Kate Munro brought back that niggling worry. What on earth had she and her friends from Ladymount been celebrating in Take Two yesterday? What had they been so jubilant about?

Once again a feeling of foreboding gripped her. It was not helped by the heavy black clouds that came over during the dinner hour.

All afternoon it poured with rain, ruling out any chance of swimming in the school pool that day. Sara felt bleak during afternoon lessons. If only Leggy were a bit more cheerful! But she sat at the next desk, sunk in her own secret gloom, hardly glancing Sara's way all afternoon.

As Sara cycled home through the rain her feeling of foreboding returned. The local evening newspaper was lying on the mat when she got indoors. It looked grey and damp and uninteresting. She picked it up and put it on the hall table. But after she had hung up her wet things some instinct brought her back to the table.

Gingerly she picked up the damp newspaper and turned to the sports pages at the back. There was a small headline, tucked near the bottom of the page. She had been expecting something like this all along, but it still gave her a dull shock:

Ladymount Girl Should Win Big Swim Again

Sara read the news item three times to make sure, but it was perfectly straightforward. There had been an inter-school swimming match at Ladymount School the previous afternoon. Kate Munro had beaten her own previous Junior County Record for the 100 metres free style. She had swum it in exactly 63 seconds.

'What's the point of going on, Davy?' asked Sara half an hour later. 'What hope have I got?'

After tea she had gone straight round to Davy's house with the offending newspaper. She had sat quietly while he read the report, but now she gave vent to her dismay.

'To think I was so pleased with myself to break through sixty-seven seconds. How Kate Munro would laugh if she knew! Sixty-three seconds. Think of it, Davy! That's faster than Tommy used to swim.'

He ran his hand through his hair several times, lost for words.

'It's a bit depressing isn't it?' He went to the kitchen. 'Wait here – there's a pot of tea just made.'

They drank tea together at the bottom of the stairs.

'Look here, Titch. You mustn't let this get you down. It's two weeks till the big swim, isn't it? If you could clip just four seconds off your time between now and then—'

'If.' All the same, Sara cheered up. 'It doesn't sound so bad when you put it like that.' Then she shook her head. 'If only I had someone really fast to race against.'

'I know. I've been racking my brains all day to think of someone. I wish I could help.' Davy cupped his hands and took an imaginary catch. 'Now if it were cricket—!'

They talked for half an hour. Davy was a great comfort. Slowly he built up some of her lost confidence. He convinced her that even now, nothing was impossible.

'And Titch,' he said, when she was ready to leave, 'how would you like to forget all about swimming just for one day?'

'What do you mean?'

'Jeff and I are going sailing at Huntsea on Saturday. Like to come?'

'Davy!' She could hardly find words to reply. Sailing was one of Davy's private, masculine pursuits. She had never been invited before. 'What would Jeff say? I'd only get in the way—'

'He won't mind. You can be our head cook and bottle-washer for the day. Come on! It'll do you good.'

'Okay,' replied Sara, trying not to look too eager.

She went to school the next day feeling more cheerful. It was a fine day, which meant there would be swimming. She was going to let Kate Munro's new time be a spur to her, not a defeat. And on Saturday she was going to the sea with Davy and Jeff, going sailing with them. A great honour!

Her feeling of wellbeing increased when she saw Leggy, just before assembly. The tall girl's withdrawn mood had quite disappeared.

'Hello, Sara. Lovely day!'

'Hi, Leggy.'

Sara stared. Leggy looked so different this morning – positively attractive. There was colour in her cheeks, she held her shoulders almost square, and the sparkle in her eyes made her look a warm, friendly person. Sara had caught glimpses of her like this before, when they had made jokes and giggled together, but the look had always quickly disappeared.

Today the girl seemed bathed in happiness. Everyone noticed it and felt more friendly towards her. Terry Horn had even picked up a book for her when she dropped it, on the way over to the Chemistry Lab.

It was all to do with a letter she had received in the morning's post. Several times during lessons Sara saw her reading the letter through, secretly, under cover of her desk.

'You've had a nice letter?' she asked, at dinner-time.

'Very,' said Leggy. But that was all. In spite of her happiness she seemed, as always, somewhere removed. Much of the time it seemed as though only her body were here at Hocking School, her thoughts far away.

'I had a nasty shock last night,' said Sara, changing the subject. She longed to penetrate the mystery that surrounded Leggy; she was the oddest person that she had ever met. But she did not want to drive her away by prying into her private affairs. 'Kate Munro's producing some fantastic swimming at the moment.'

She told Leggy about it, as lightly as she could.

'Yes, I knew you had some way to go yet,' said the tall girl sagely. 'You won't improve your performance overnight, but in two weeks you might just do it. Your leg action is the key to everything. The more consistent you keep your leg action, the faster you'll go. But to do it you've got to tune up your leg muscles, and that means some really hard work.'

Once more Sara was surprised by the calm authority in Leggy's voice.

CHAPTER SEVEN

Off to the Sea

At the end of the afternoon Sara had a swimming session and a few minutes' coaching with Tommy. The teacher, too, had been dismayed by the item in the local paper, but she concealed her feelings well.

'You could be the person to worry her, Sara, if you carry on improving like this,' she said firmly.

They concentrated entirely on 'breath holding'. After a while, Tommy glanced at her watch. She was due to umpire a tennis match.

'I've got to go now, but stay and practise that. It helps you sprint at the beginning and end of a race if you can hold your breath for two or more stroke cycles. You're giving a firmer base from which the propelling muscles of your arms can work.'

Sara swam a length, concentrating hard. She touched the side and lifted her head from the water. There was someone towering above her, in skirt and blazer, arms folded with cool detachment. Now that the teacher had gone she had suddenly appeared like a genie from a magic lamp.

'Leggy!'

'Forget about your breathing now,' said Leggy. 'You've got to tune up those muscles if you want to be a *real* swimmer. Here, grab the rail at the side and let yourself float on your tummy.'

Meekly, Sara obeyed.

'Right. I'm going to start counting, while you leg kick in time. Start your kicks right up in the hip, not at the knee. Keep your legs close together. I'm warning you, Sara. Your legs will feel like murder tomorrow. But you've got to do this – for your own sake.'

She counted and her voice reverberated round the deserted school swimming pool. Down in the water, gripping the rail with outstretched arms, Sara pretended that her legs were scarcely able to bend at the knee.

'One – two, one – two, up – down, up – down, one – two . . .'

As the voice beat on relentlessly, Sara's muscles began to ache.

'Your knees are bending too much! Your legs are sinking lower in the water. Up! Up! Keep them up – no, that's too high! Only your heels should break water. One – two. One – two.'

Kick – kick, kick – kick. Would the agony never end? wondered Sara. 'Okay. Rest!'

She let her feet touch the bottom and leant against the side of the bath, panting for breath. She could see Leggy's feet and long skinny legs towering above her.

'I should come out now. That's probably enough for the first time.'

Sara hadn't even the strength to lift herself up over the side of the swimming pool. She came out by the steps and then limped over to her changing cubicle, ashamed to let Leggy see her in such a knocked-out state.

She sank down on the bench, wrapped in a towel. She must have sat there for quite some time, because suddenly Leggy's face appeared over the top of the door, peering in at her.

'You've a long way to go,' she said knowledgeably. 'You've got to do this exercise at least once a day if you really want to tune up your leg muscles. That's where Kate Munro's got the edge on you – legs. She's got such a beautiful leg action it never falters, so her body's always streamlined in the water. That's one reason why she's so fast.'

'How do you know that?' asked Sara in dull surprise.

'I–' Leggy paused. 'I saw her swim once, in a County race. Mind if I dash now? I'm late for tea.'

The tall girl vanished as suddenly as she had arrived. Alone, Sara felt limp and rather cold. She got dressed, collected her bike, and made for home.

She woke up the next morning feeling rather depressed. She stretched.

'Ouch!'

Cycling to school with Davy he knew at once that something was wrong. Sara winced every time her feet pressed down on the pedals.

'Something wrong with your legs?'

'They're killing me.'

Ruefully she told him about Leggy's sudden appearance at the school pool – and the unexpected 'coaching session'.

'She really put me through it, I can tell you. What a slave-driver!'

'What does she know about it?' asked Davy, annoyed. Then, musing as they cycled along, his indignation grew. 'What a weird-o she is! Can't swim a stroke herself – frightened of the water – gets you to risk your neck and forge a note from her mother . . .'

'She didn't "get" me to at all!' protested Sara. 'I felt sorry for her.'

'All right,' Davy conceded. 'But I still think she's got a nerve.'

'Aren't you forgetting something?' asked Sara gently. 'It works. I mean – I've done under sixty-seven seconds, following Leggy's advice. She *does* seem to know what she's talking about!'

She winced as she pedalled the last steep bit in through

the school gates and for the first time an irreverent voice whispered inside her: *All this because you want to beat Kate Munro in the Jane Cup! Is it worth it – is it really?*

However, as the day wore on at school, Sara's spirits rose. The ache in her legs started to ebb away. It was a bright, clear day. She got an 'A' for History homework from Miss Phipps, and the weekend lay ahead. With a warm glow of anticipation she was counting the hours now to her day at Huntsea with Davy and Jeff.

Perhaps best of all, Leggy was still in the glowing good humour that had started with the mysterious letter she had received the previous morning. Gone was the sullen aloofness which brought out the worst in Terry Horn and his friends. She was still withdrawn, her mind elsewhere, but at least her cheeks glowed and her eyes were bright.

There was a swimming lesson that afternoon and Leggy, excused games as usual, sat on the terrace of the school pool reading a book with studied nonchalance. She appeared to take little interest in the swimming, but she glanced up when Tommy button-holed Sara at the end of the lesson.

'Your leg action is looking up,' said the PE teacher with a brisk nod. 'That was something I wanted to work on, but you seem to be working on it yourself.'

Sara glanced at Leggy. She had felt a new confidence in the water today, the beginnings of a sensation of body balance that she had never known existed. If only she could tell Tommy that the tall, spindly 'invalid' sitting nearby deserved the credit for the improvement! She contented herself by exchanging a secret smile with Leggy. And said, innocently:

'Is it really?'

She saw Leggy, briefly, at the end of the afternoon. The tall girl had raced to get her things after lessons, and was humming happily in the cloakroom.

'Have a nice weekend, Sara.'

'I will. You have a nice one, too.'

'Don't worry, I will!' laughed Leggy. 'I'm looking forward to it no end!'

Sara watched her as she fled out of the school building like a bird released from a cage. She combed her hair, slowly. What went on in Leggy's private life that produced such dramatic ups and downs in her moods? Perhaps the letter she had received was connected with some kind of invitation for the weekend.

'Has she got a boy-friend?' wondered Sara – and then she shook her head decisively. She cycled home, mentally going through her wardrobe and trying on one outfit after another. Just what should she wear for the day's sailing with Davy? Her flowered cotton trouser suit, or just denim jeans and a shirt?

She wore the jeans, in the end, with a brightly striped t-shirt, selected with much thought and care. Davy, of course, didn't even notice what she was wearing.

'Got your goggles and flippers, Titch?' he asked, when she got round to his house early the next morning.

'No!' replied Sara. 'You said I was to forget all about swimming for one day.'

'That's right,' remembered Davy. 'I meant racing-type swimming. There's no reason why we shouldn't have some fun.' He looked out of the window; there was an early mist, but the dew on the front lawn was steaming. 'It's going to be hot. Jeff thought you might like it if we sailed round from Huntsea to Southdene Cove. It's a great place for underwater swimming.'

'Oooh. I would like that,' decided Sara. 'I'll just nip home and get them.'

She came out of her house five minutes later with her goggles and flippers under her arm, just in time to see Jeff's old car pull up outside Davy's house. The car was painted a vivid yellow, with various slogans all over it. Jeff, who was quite a bit older than his cousin Davy, had passed his driving test a month ago and gone straight out and bought a banger.

For two weekends running Sara had seen the boys painting the car outside Davy's house and felt slightly envious of their private, masculine world. She had never imagined that she would soon be getting this invitation to join them for a day's sailing. Even now she felt slightly nervous and shy of Jeff and wondered if he really approved of Davy's impulsive invitation to her, when she had been feeling depressed. She need not have worried.

'Climb in, Titch,' ordered Jeff. 'I hear you're going to be head of catering, for the day.'

'That's right,' said Sara. She pointed to the picnic basket that Davy was loading into the back of the car. 'Only I've done all the chores in advance. There's everything we need in there, I've even baked a cake.'

'Good girl.'

She enjoyed the twenty-mile drive to Huntsea. They went by a pretty route through country lanes and soon the sun came out and Davy reached above his head. After much heaving and straining, he managed to pull the rusty sunshine roof open as they drove along. Sara leant back, relaxed, and let the breeze ruffle her hair and the sun bathe her cheeks in warmth.

'What a super car, Jeff,' she said.

CHAPTER EIGHT

Mistaken Identity

At Huntsea, they parked down by the harbour, where the boys kept their boat. There were a lot of sailing-boats moored in the harbour, some of them quite magnificent. Men, tanned and denim-trousered, were up and about, working on their boats. A tall Bermuda-rig sailing-boat was already putting out of the harbour towards the open sea. It had bright red sails and was flying through the sparkling blue sea directly into the sun, so that it was almost in silhouette. It was a superb sight and Sara drew in her breath.

They carried the picnic basket and all their swimming equipment down the worn stone steps inside the harbour wall. Next to a large white cabin-cruiser a small sailing dinghy bobbed on the water. It looked very insignificant to the casual observer, but not to Davy and Jeff. It was their very own boat, which they had built together the previous summer, and they gazed at it with loving pride.

'So that's *Helen of Troy*!' exclaimed Sara. 'I've heard so much about her. She's lovely.'

Davy's father had teased them constantly when they were building the boat.

'As soon as she takes to sea, every lifeboat for miles around will be on the alert,' he had joked. 'You ought to call her "*Helen of Troy* – the boat that launched a thousand ships".'

The dinghy was perfectly seaworthy, as it turned out, but the name had stuck.

'Just as beautiful as the original Helen,' said Jeff.

They loaded their stuff aboard and the boys started to unfurl the mainsail.

When Davy gave the word, Sara untied the mooring-rope and jumped aboard.

There was a good stiff breeze blowing and soon they were heading for the open sea, Jeff at the tiller, handling the mainsail, Davy handling the small jibsail, and Sara acting as ballast. Her job was to duck under the mainsail from time to time, leaning backwards over the side of the boat, first to starboard, then to port, as they tacked out to sea. It was not a very skilful job, but quite tiring. Sara was glad when, a mile out at sea, the boys set sail on an even course, running before the wind. Now she could just sit still next to Jeff in the stern and enjoy the sensation of the wind blowing into her back and the salt spray splashing up at her arms.

'Isn't this fun!' she exclaimed. 'Who'd have dreamt we could go so fast!'

'The wind's well up,' nodded Jeff. 'Think you could like sailing?'

'I'm sure I could!' she laughed, and meant it. It was glorious to be speeding through the blue water, yet so silently, without engines. The land looked far away and hazy, and the only sound was the lashing of the water and the cry of a seagull wheeling above them. 'Is that a headland over there?'

In the distance a long finger of land was curling round to meet them and Jeff, fractionally altering course, headed straight towards it. As they got nearer, Sara saw a beautiful big cove encircled by cliffs. On top of the cliffs were some long low white buildings, gleaming in the morning light.

'That's Southdene Cove, where we're going to do some underwater stuff!' yelled Davy. 'And that's Southdene School on top of the cliffs.'

'Of course – the girls' boarding-school. I've never seen it from this angle before!'

As they came into the sheltered waters of the large cove, they lost a lot of wind and had to begin tacking again, careful to zig-zag well clear of an outcrop of rocks. There were several boats in the cove and a lot of people were swimming. They drew in the sail and decided to moor out from the shore, alongside a long line of rocks. A girl was lying on her back on the rocks, sunbathing. She wore a dark blue bathing costume with the white monogram of Southdene School.

Tall and graceful, the girl raised herself languidly on one elbow as they approached. Sara stared at her face in astonishment.

'I must be seeing things,' she gasped. 'It's Leggy!'

'Eh?' frowned Davy. He was struggling to secure *Helen of Troy*'s mooring rope in a firm bowline knot round a spar of rock. The waters of Southdene Cove seemed calm enough but here by the line of rocks there was a swirling undercurrent, enough to make the boat bob backwards and forwards. The rope kept jerking and twisting in Davy's hands.

'Let's take her farther in,' said Jeff.

The boys let the boat drift in close to the sandy beach. Sara watched as the elegant figure sunbathing on the rocks receded from them. Dimly she was aware of the boys tying up the boat to a breakwater, close inshore. She was unable to take her eyes off that distant figure in dark blue.

'It's Leggy, I tell you,' she repeated dumbfounded.

'Who?' asked Davy. Now that the boat was secure, he took an interest at last. 'You mean that graceful-looking bird stretched out on the rocks back there? Don't be daft, Titch. I know you always look on the bright side as far as

Leggy's concerned, but even you can't imagine she's got a figure like that in a bathing suit.'

'Leggy?' exclaimed Jeff, whose keen eyes had not overlooked the impeccable shape back there. He cottoned on to the fact that they were talking about Sara's new friend at Hocking School. He laughed and whistled. 'If *that's* what she looks like, Davy, I can't see what you've got against her. But it can't be of course. Didn't you notice, Sara? She's wearing a Southdene swim-suit.'

'I know,' said Sara. She was slipping off her life jacket and rolling up her jeans. 'That's what's so extraordinary But it's Leggy all right – I've never been so sure of anything. I'm going back to say hello.'

She lowered herself over the side of the boat and waded through the shallows to where the long line of rocks came right into shore. She pulled herself up on to the rocks. The damp, grey stone, soft with seaweed in places, felt good beneath her bare feet. Nimbly she raced along the pier of rock, back out to sea, dodging round the deep clear pools of seawater that the receding tide had left amongst the hollows of the rocks.

'Leggy! Leggy!'

Davy and Jeff stayed in the boat, tying in the sails and watching Sara run into the distance. Their curiosity was aroused.

'Leggy!' gasped Sara.

The tall girl on the rocks was in a sitting position now. She had taken an apple from the picnic box beside her and was munching it. She sat there on a bright yellow towel, idly surveying the swimmers out in the cove. Beyond the picnic box sat a big pile of clothes; for a moment Sara believed she recognized Leggy's favourite brown sandals amongst them.

'I beg your pardon?'

The tall girl turned her head and surveyed Sara, who was breathless and dishevelled. She had big clear eyes and a beautiful complexion which gave her face a compelling radiance. Not a hair was out of place. Sara felt scruffy and suddenly very ill at ease. For the first time a tiny shadow of doubt crept into her mind. Her cheeks began to go red.

It was Leggy's face – the same eyes, the same eyebrows; even the nose was exactly the same. The mouth, too, was quite unmistakable. It was Leggy's face – and at the same time it wasn't. The ever-present spectacles were missing. So was the haughty, withdrawn, rather lonely look. This was the face of a girl who enjoyed life, in a relaxed and self-confident way. It was the face of a popular girl, someone who had plenty of friends. Here was a girl who attracted people like a magnet, while the Leggy that Sara knew positively drove people away.

She had Leggy's build, too. The same amazing height in someone so young, the same long limbs and bony shoulders. Yet the grace and confidence of the face spread right through the girl's body. She looked slender and graceful, where Leggy looked skinny and gawky. Her shoulders were held straight, not rounded.

'I – I –' stuttered Sara. 'I thought you looked like someone I knew—'

'Viv! Viv! 'squealed some voices from the water.

Three girls were swimming strongly towards the rocks, waving and laughing. They all wore the regulation swimsuits of Southdene School and were coming this way.

'What are you doing loafing on the rocks?'

'Come in, Viv – do!'

'It's delicious!'

The girl called Vivienne gave Sara an interested glance and then turned away, smiling apologetically.

'Do excuse me – friends of mine.'

She ran lightly over the rocks and crouched down, talking to the friends who swarmed round her, Sara's presence completely forgotten. Hot with embarrassment now, Sara turned away and walked slowly back along the rocks the way she had come, staring resolutely down at her feet as she walked.

The boys watched her coming and roared with laughter. Her discomfiture stood out clearly, even from this distance. They helped her back into the boat.

'You boobed, Sara!' grinned Davy. 'Never mind.'

'You can say that again,' said Sara, running her hands through her hair in perplexity. 'But the likeness was amazing – it really was.'

CHAPTER NINE

The Mystery Swimmer

Davy had been right when he said it was going to be hot that Saturday.The sun rose up and up in the sky, casting a great heat. They decided to spend the whole day in Southdene Cove.

'Sailing's for all weathers,' declared Jeff. 'It's not every day we can swim and dive and sunbathe – or else – ' he eyed the big picnic basket hungrily ' – just relax and stuff ourselves.'

'You're right, Jeff,' said Sara, but there must have been just a twinge of regret in her voice.

'I do believe Sara's getting hooked on sailing,' laughed Davy.

'Then she can come with us again,' said Jeff firmly.

'Really?' asked Sara, in delight. Now her happiness was complete.

They had a short swim in the cove, just to cool off and get up an appetite for lunch. Then, in a quiet corner of the sandy cove, their backs against the cliff wall, they unpacked the picnic basket. Sara had baked lots of sausage rolls as well as a cake, and had made up sandwiches too.

She poured iced coffee from a Thermos flask into three mugs while the boys tucked in to the food.

'Mmmm,' said Davy.

'You can *certainly* come again!' said Jeff, grabbing his third sausage roll with such gusto that some of the crisp brown pastry flaked into the sand.

They finished off the meal with cheese and fruit and

then sank back exhausted. The sun was so hot now that they had to move into more shade. The boys lazed and talked about boats for a while and then got to their feet.

'We're just going to walk that lot off, Sara.'

She smiled and started to tidy up the picnic things, doing the washing up at the edge of the sea. She watched the boys as they walked round the cove, admiring some of the sailing-boats moored along the shore and talking to fellow enthusiasts. Once she stared across the pier of rock on the far side of the cove, where she had had her encounter with Leggy's 'double'. She thought she could still see her there, joined by another girl, a tall girl in a white bathing suit.

'Come on, Sara, get your goggles and flippers,' said Davy, when they returned.

The three of them walked across the sand and over some rocks to where a formation of craggy grey rocks formed a huge rock pool that was perfectly circular and very deep.

'This is *the* place for underwater swimming,' explained Jeff. 'Keep your eyes open when you dive down to the sea bed, there's tons to see.'

Feeling very content, Sara put on her rubber flippers and goggles. She was a good underwater swimmer, but she had never been to this spot before.

She climbed on a rock, took a deep breath, and dived. She swooped down, down into the water, her eyes wide open behind her watertight goggles. It was a journey from one world to another. For a few seconds she drifted along on the sandy bed, staring at the fishes and the abundance of plants that grew there. She glimpsed a beautiful big white shell, lying in the sand, reached out for it and missed. She then swam rapidly up to the surface gasping for air.

There were at least a dozen people here underwater swimming and she didn't want anyone else to find the magnificent shell. She rested for a few moments and then dived again. This time she came down in the wrong place and couldn't even see the shell.

As she rested on the rocks, preparing to make her third dive, she became aware of a tall girl in a white swim-suit and red bathing hat. The girl was wearing goggles and flippers like herself and was repeatedly diving down as though searching for something.

'She's after *my* shell,' Sara thought. 'I just know it.'

Davy and Jeff came splashing past in their goggles and flippers.

'Davy thinks he's seen a dogfish!' yelled Jeff. 'He's trying to spear it!'

But she only had eyes for that tall, lean girl swimmer. She watched in admiration as the girl executed a magnificent dive and swooped down into the sea at speed.

'And that's where the shell is!' muttered Sara. She stretched up high, arms above her head, and took in a long deep breath. Then she dived.

There was a rush of water about her ears as she shot down towards the sea-bed. Through her goggles she could see the white shape of her rival, distorted like an image in a fairground mirror, floating on her front along the sea-bed, looking this way and that, arms outstretched. She looked like a phantom.

Sara saw the shell first. She landed almost exactly on top of it and, with triumph, reached out her arm and let her hand close over it. Got it!

Then, quite suddenly, the white-suited figure sprinted across to her, grabbed her wrist and prised the shell out of her hand. It all happened so quickly that Sara, taken completely by surprise, relinquished the shell without a struggle. She saw the girl shoot up towards the surface and only then did she realize fully that her prize had been stolen from her.

She surfaced like a cork popping from a champagne bottle, gulping in air. She saw the back view of her rival, already out of the water, scrambling over the rocks that encircled the pool.

Sara swam across in pursuit, the blood pounding in her temples angrily. She clambered over the rocks in time to see the girl make a long low racing dive into the open sea. The girl was now breaking into a strong crawl, heading for the opposite side of the cove.

'Hey!' gasped Sara. 'That's *my* shell! I'm not going to let you get away with it.'

She did her best sprint dive into the sea and swam strongly in pursuit of the girl. It was good to know that she was the fastest Junior swimmer at Hocking School and she felt a moment's gratitude for the coaching that Leggy had given her. She was conscious of the new power in her swimming today. She would soon overtake this clown and insist on having her shell back!

On on, she swam, out into the middle of the cove. She could feel herself moving powerfully through the water and she knew that she was knocking up a good speed. Yet, with chagrin, she soon realized that she was unable to narrow the gap between herself and her rival.

'This girl really can swim!' thought Sara. 'Who is she?'

She really had to egg herself on now. Keeping up speed in a cross-current was a lot more exhausting than in the calm waters of the school swimming pool. She had been confident of catching the girl after a few yards, but soon they were almost across the entire width of Southdene Cove and still her rival was well ahead. Both girls were aided by their flippers, but even so they had crossed the cove at a very good pace. Sara's limbs were starting to get weary. The sea-water seemed to get heavier with every stroke now, and her leg action was slowing down.

'Light-fingered Lucy is easing up, too,' Sara realized. 'At least she's human, then. But I'm never going to catch her now.'

She slowed right down. She switched from the crawl to the more relaxing breast-stroke. A feeling of exhaustion came over her, and her anger ebbed away.

'Oh, blow her,' she decided. 'Let her keep the rotten old shell, if it means so much to her. I feel so tired now it doesn't seem to matter any more.'

The girl had reached the long pier of flat rocks that reached out to sea on the far side of the cove. She was very near the spot where Sara had encountered Leggy's 'double'.

Sara trod water lazily, her chest heaving as she slowly recovered her breath. She watched as the tall swimmer pulled herself up out of the sea on to a flat ledge of rock and sat there for a while, getting her wind back.

All this time, the girl had no idea that she had been pursued across the cove.

'I haven't the strength to argue with her about the shell,' Sara thought. Idly she let herself drift towards the seated girl. It was curiosity and not anger that pulled her onwards now. 'Who is she? I'd love to know. She's a great swimmer – but perhaps she's a lot older than me. Two or three years at least.'

Yet Sara's instinct told her that this was as not so. The girl somehow seemed about her own age and what was more there was something indefinably familiar about her, underneath that tight red bathing hat and the large pair of goggles that covered the top half of her face.

'I know her, I'm sure I do.' The definite feeling of having seen the girl before increased as Sara drew nearer. She now had a strong compulsion to discover who she was. 'I'll just drift in here, behind these rocks.'

She allowed a wave to take her in between two spurs of rock, and then gingerly she heaved herself out of the water on to a narrow ledge. It was good to sit on the firm ledge and lean her aching back against the slab of rock behind her. For a few moments she let every muscle sag as the salt water ran off her body into little dripping pools all around her. The sun bathed her in warmth and her breath was coming more easily now. What a pace that girl had set across the cove!

Sara stared back across the water to the large rock pool on the far side of the cove; she could just make out the tiny figures of Davy and Jeff, towelling themselves down on a rock. It was amazing that she had swum all this way in such a short time.

Silently she removed her goggles and flippers. Then—

'Eve! Eve! Here – grab a towel!'

As that voice rang out, Sara got to her feet and peered over the top of the rock which concealed her. She felt as though she were having a dream.

Just a few yards away the tall girl in the white swimming suit had risen eagerly to her feet to greet someone who was running lightly over the rocks to meet her. It was the graceful girl in the blue Southdene School swimsuit whom she had encountered earlier, the girl called Vivienne. Her eyes were sparkling in her sun-tanned face and her hair was billowing. She was holding out a large towel as she advanced.

The other girl, who had her back to Sara, had taken off her goggles.

'Viv! I've got something for you.'

Sara's thoughts began to tumble around in her head as she recognized that voice.

CHAPTER TEN

A Fierce Quarrel

'It can wait, Eve my love! You're shivering – that was quite some swim. Here, come over here and I'll give you a rub down.'

The girl in the white suit took the towel and wrapped it round her shoulders and then the two of them padded away over the rocks to their pile of belongings. Silently Sara pulled herself up over the tall slab of rock, jumped down on the other side, and crept after them. She was not in the habit of deliberately spying on people but this was different. She had to see if she were right, see it with her own eyes.

She dropped down behind a shoulder of rock, near the picnic box and the pile of clothes where she had encountered Vivienne that morning. She had a clear back view of the two girls as they sat down on the warm rocks and the one began to rub the other briskly with the towel.

'Here, take your hat off, let's give your hair a rub.'

The red swimming hat was tugged off and the familiar brown hair cascaded down, damp at the edges. The girl started to rummage around amongst the clothes, groping for something.

'Your specs? Here they are.'

'Thanks, Viv. I'm whacked. I'm out of practice, no doubt about it.'

'Don't you do any swimming at that school then?'

'No – no decent competition,' the girl replied, then changed the subject. 'Wait till you see what I've got you!'

She was groping down the front of her swim-suit. Triumphantly she brought out the huge, gleaming white shell. 'I found it on the sea-bed. It took quite some getting, I can tell you.'

'Oh, Eve. It – it's beautiful. It'll look wonderful with the others.'

'That's what I thought. There was another girl after it. But I saw it first and I was so determined to get it for your collection.'

'She didn't chase you, did she?'

'Chase me?'

'Oh, I thought I saw a girl swimming after you across the cove just now.'

The girl in spectacles turned round for the first time, gazing out across the sea, looking at the water keenly. She shook her head. In her hiding-place, Sara drew in a very deep breath. For the first time she had a crystal-clear view of the girl's face.

'It's Leggy all right,' she thought. 'Vivienne is her twin sister.'

A sense of outrage and anger was welling up like a fountain inside her. She thought:

'She's lied to me. The conceited, stuck-up snob – she can swim like a fish!'

Limp with shock, she could not move a muscle.

Leggy was getting dressed now, all the time gazing happily at her twin sister. She was bathed in contentment; there was not a hint of the sulkiness and bad temper that was so often in evidence at Hocking School. It was as though she were a mirror and, in the presence of her sister, she took on Vivienne's qualities of happiness and self-confidence.

'I'm so glad you like the shell,' she was saying. 'I've been hoping to find something like this for you today, Viv. It's a sort of memento of the wonderful day we've had together. When you look at it, it'll remind you of our reunion. You will look at it, won't you, Viv?' she pleaded. 'Look at it and think about me – send out nice thought waves, and I'll send some back.'

Even in her numb state, Sara noted that Vivienne was visibly embarrassed by her sister's outpouring.

'Er – yes – of course I will, Eve. But don't go on so.'

'No, of course not, Viv. I – I'm sorry. I'm talking too much. I'm being silly. It's just that – oh, Viv—' With her twin sister's slight reprimand, Leggy's new-found confidence was visibly slipping away, and she buried her face in her hands. 'We've never been apart before, and I miss you so much.'

'Of course you do. We miss each other.' Vivienne was rising to her feet, patting Leggy's hair and talking in a soothing way, as one might humour a child. At the same time she was glancing at her watch. 'But we've got to fly now, both of us. I'm due back at school for tea – and you're going to miss your coach if you don't look out.'

The twins collected up their things and, fully dressed now, set off at a brisk pace along the pier of rocks towards the beach. Sara followed them, trembling a little.

She had tried not to eavesdrop on their private conversation, but inevitably she had got the gist of it. At that time she did not concern herself with Leggy's feelings, or see any pathos in the situation. She was far too angry at the way she had been deceived, and her anger was all the worse for having to be bottled up. It was out of the question to make a scene in front of Vivienne.

'All the efforts I've made to be friends with her!' Sara thought. 'And she never really wanted my friendship at all. She's completely wrapped up in that twin of hers – I can see it all now.' She stared up at the long low buildings of Southdene School, there on the cliffs above the cove.

'Vivienne goes to that super boarding-school, and she wishes she did too. She hates Hocking School!'

She followed the girls as they crossed the beach and then, by a coach stop on the promenade, they stopped. They spoke for a few moments, hugged and said good-bye, and then Vivienne went hurrying off up the cliff road in the direction of Southdene School.

Leggy was left standing by the coach stop, waving and waving until her sister was out of sight. Sara climbed up off the beach, her goggles and flippers under her arm, feeling rather under-dressed with only her swim-suit on but not caring.

'Leggy!'

She approached the girl from behind. She had stopped waving now and was staring into space, her shoulders hunched up and dejected. Sara touched her on her back.

'Leggy!'

She spun round and looked into Sara's face, not recognizing her for a moment, for her vision was misted up and her eyes were blurred with tears. Then—

'Sara—' she gasped, uncomprehendingly.

'Recognize me?' she asked sarcastically. 'You jolly well ought to. You grabbed a shell out of my hand, over at the rock pool.'

'Oh – it – it was you?' Leggy could hardly take it in. 'I never dreamt! Oh, Sara, I don't usually go around doing things like that. I – I'm sorry—'

'You did it for that sister of yours – you'd do anything for her!' Sara's anger was finding its release now. 'I'm sorry, Leggy, I've found out a lot about you in the past half-hour. You – you liar! To think I liked you and wanted to help you find your feet at Hocking! When you said you couldn't swim and were scared of the water, I believed you! You let me take risks for you – forging that note to get you out of swimming – and all the time—'

Sara, trying to control her emotions, spoke slowly and deliberately:

'All the time you could swim like a fish – better than me! How you must have been laughing behind my back! You didn't *want* to swim – you didn't want to join in things at Hocking School – you're far too superior. You're just as stuck up and horrible as everyone believes—'

A shadow loomed over them as a coach slowed down at the stop.

'I'm going,' said Leggy, and she was pale and trembling. 'I'm not going to listen to another word.'

'Go by all means,' snapped Sara. She felt spent by her outburst. 'Frankly, I wouldn't care if I never saw you again.'

The two girls stood in shadow. The big red coach that ran inland to Hocking was towering above them at the bus stop. One or two people had alighted and the driver was waiting patiently at the wheel, his eyebrows slightly raised at the sight of two girls quarrelling by the door of his coach. There was the little pretty one, barefoot, wearing only a bathing suit, squaring up to the tall, skinny one in glasses who wore a summer dress and brown sandals, with a duffel-bag looped over her arm.

'You don't know what you're talking about, Sara,' said Leggy, quietly. 'You just don't understand.'

'There's nothing to understand,' retorted Sara. 'You hate Hocking School. You never wanted to be my friend. You've lied from start to finish about not being able to swim. You can't be *bothered* to swim at our school because you reckon none of us are good enough for you. I heard you tell your sister—'

'I'm not listening,' said Leggy, once again. 'Believe what you want to believe. It's not like that at all.'

'Come on, miss, if you're coming,' shouted the coach driver.

Leggy turned her back on Sara and jumped aboard; a second later the push-button doors snapped shut behind her and the coach slid away from the bus stop.

Sara watched it go. It bumped and bounced along the promenade and then turned off to the right, away from the sea front, and disappeared from view. Only the smell of exhaust fumes remained. Leggy had gone.

She passed a hand across her forehead and realized that she was shivering slightly, standing there in her swim-suit. She walked back to the stone steps that led down on to the beach. Soon she was walking barefoot across the sand, back to the deep rock pool where she had left Davy and Jeff half an hour ago.

CHAPTER ELEVEN

A Long Talk with Davy

'Sara! Where did you get to?'

Head down as she walked along, she had almost bumped into the two boys. They were dressed now, carrying the picnic things, and had obviously been looking for her. Davy was looking straight at her and smiling.

'Been having some sly swimming practice, I suppose?' he said. 'This was supposed to be a day off for you, champion.'

'Champion!' retorted Sara. 'I'm not even the fastest at Hocking School, not any longer!'

'What are you talking about?' Davy asked. 'Sounds very mysterious.'

'It's a long story,' sighed Sara. She shook her head.

'Okay. You must tell it to us sometime.' Davy realized that she was in no mood to talk. He was carrying her jeans and striped t-shirt under his arm, rolled up. 'Here, slip these on. You'll catch a cold. Besides – we've got to get going.'

Jeff was staring out to sea. He licked his forefinger and held it up.

'Wind's dropping fast, Titch. We've got to get back to Huntsea now, or we'll find we're becalmed.'

They waited on the sand while Sara put her clothes on over her swim-suit, which was now completely dry. Then the three of them walked briskly back to the spot where they had moored the *Helen of Troy*. There was plenty of work to be done, and not much time for talking. Sara threw herself into helping the boys with the rigging, relieved not to have to think about – or talk about – anything.

Soon they were tacking slowly out to sea, away from Southdene Cove, the mainsail flapping rather limply in the feeble breeze.

'It's going to take much longer going back,' observed Jeff. 'Not like this morning.'

Sara remembered how buoyant she had felt that morning, and how the sail had billowed full, racing them here. Now, just like *Helen of Troy*'s sail, she felt deflated. It was all thanks to Leggy. Her anger had gone, but not the sense of betrayal and hurt.

It took them over an hour just to get round the headland. They kept close to the coastline and, once round, a little bit of breeze whipped up and helped them across to Huntsea. The small seaside resort looked warm and still in a haze of late afternoon sunshine.

It was nearly six o'clock when they tied up at the boat's permanent mooring in Huntsea Harbour. Sara set to work to brew up tea on the Primus stove in the little cabin. The hot drink tasted good and they ate the remains of their picnic.

'That's better,' said Jeff, who had been hungry. 'Who's for home?'

They bounced back along the country lanes to Hocking, in the old car. They sang songs at the tops of their voices, and Sara's spirits revived.

They pulled up in front of her house.

'It's been a good day, hasn't it?' said Jeff.

'Yes – of course,' smiled Sara. She collected up her things.

'You will come with us again?'

'You bet!'

Davy saw her to her front door.

'You know I want to hear all about it, Sara. What

happened this afternoon? Something did happen, didn't it?'

'Yes, Davy,' she replied. 'But it *has* been a good day. I think sailing's fabulous. I'd love to do it again! As for the other business – I'll tell you tomorrow.'

'Good. We'll go out for a ride on our bikes. I'll call for you after dinner.'

'Fine!' Sara's face showed she meant it. 'I'll see you then, Davy.'

Next day, when he called for her, she felt a sense of quiet anticipation. It would be interesting to confide in him about the whole extraordinary Leggy business.

An hour later, sucking a stem of grass, he said flatly:

'I never took to her from the start, and that's a fact.'

The two friends had cycled to the top of Hocking Hill and were now lazing in the park, their bikes propped against a dead elm tree. Sara gazed towards the glade where they had encountered Leggy for the very first time. She remembered her with the flower, her eyes glittering behind her spectacles as though the world were hateful.

Davy followed Sara's thoughts.

'It certainly explains a few things, her having this twin sister at Southdene – and being so wrapped up in her. That's probably who she was phoning that day. Remember the way she flounced out of the phone box?'

'Just what I was thinking,' said Sara. 'She – she does miss Vivienne, that's obvious. Remember how happy she seemed at school on Friday – almost radiant? She'd had a letter. It must have been from Vivienne, fixing up for them to spend yesterday at Huntsea together.'

'It's about time she grew up,' said Davy. 'Stood on her own two feet. They're large enough.'

'I wonder *why* she's come to Hocking School on her own like this,' said Sara. 'Why aren't both girls at Southdene?'

'We can guess,' shrugged Davy. 'Southdene's a girls' public school, the fees must be astronomical. Oil sheiks' daughters from deepest Arabia and all that. Perhaps Leggy's parents can only afford for *one* of them to go there, while the other goes to the state school. I bet you anything that's why Leggy's so anti-social. She resents being at Hocking and looks down on us. She probably feels that none of us are good enough for her – and that she belongs in a place like Southdene.'

'Suppose so,' frowned Sara. This very suspicion was what made her angry. She was hurt to think that while she had been giving her friendship to the new girl, that friendship had not really been wanted. But today she was less certain. 'I hope I haven't been too hasty, though. It's terribly easy to jump to conclusions – and sometimes be wrong.'

'I don't think you're wrong about Leggy. She's not worth your friendship.'

'She doesn't want it,' said Sara, with a sigh. 'I'm convinced of that now. The funny thing is, Davy—' She could not meet his disapproving eye, and turned away as she spoke. 'There's something about her. I still like her, I really do. I still have an instinct about her – that really she's not how she seems. That underneath it all she's really *nice*.'

Davy laughed then, took Sara's hands and pulled her to her feet.

'Oh, Titch – you're impossible. I can't argue with feminine intuition. Well, at least you've got it all off your chest. Let's make a move.'

'Yes, let's,' said Sara. 'And – thanks Davy. I *have* got it off my chest, and I feel much better for it.'

'Thought any more about your chances in the big swim?' he asked.

'I think of nothing else,' said Sara, as they mounted

their bikes outside the park gates. 'I'm getting a bit faster, thanks to Leggy's coaching. But when I think about Kate Munro doing the distance in 63 seconds . . .'

'Let's see if we can spy on the competition,' said Davy.

They crossed the hill and made their way down the quiet track that led past the grounds of Kate Munro's house. As they passed near the Munros' private lake they heard the sound of laughter and tinkling glasses. Quietly they dismounted from their bikes and crept through the trees to the boundary fence. They pressed their faces against the palings and peered through.

'Look at her!'

'I'm green with envy,' confessed Sara.

There was the slim, athletic figure of Kate, stretched out on a flowered lounger at the lakeside. Her bathing suit was a brilliant white contrasting with her tanned body. Her red hair was tousled against the flowered canvas. She was taking a lemonade from a tall muscular man called Grundy, her own private swimming coach. She was surrounded by three friends from Ladymount School, all in bathing suits. They were all drinking lemonade and hanging on to her words.

'Oh, Kate!' giggled one of them in a high-pitched voice. 'You're marvellous.'

'There's that Alsatian of hers,' muttered Davy. 'The one that ripped my best pants to bits. Oh, Sara,' he sighed as they turned back to their bikes, 'I wish you could take the Jane Cup away from her. Beat the living daylights out of her.'

'So do I,' said Sara quietly. Kate Munro really was the most cocksure and conceited person she had ever met. 'She's a good swimmer all right, but she does have a few advantages that we ordinary mortals don't possess.'

'Like having Grundy to swim against all the time?'

'Yes,' sighed Sara. They free-wheeled down the track,

leaving the laughter and the tinkling glasses behind them. 'If only I could race against Tommy more. But she's so busy – she just hasn't got the time.'

'But you've *got* a racing partner now,' said Davy softly. 'Yours for the asking.'

'You mean—?' Sara turned her head and stared at him.

'I mean Leggy. She owes you that at least, after the way she's deceived you.'

'Oh, Davy – Leggy doesn't want to swim against me or anybody else. She can't be bothered. Look at the extremes she went to, to get out of swimming lessons. Letting me forge that note for her from her mother, to get her off games.'

'Precisely,' said Davy. 'You've got a hold over her, haven't you?'

'Davy!' Sara laughed.

Then, as she thought about it, 'Oh, Davy – I couldn't. I couldn't *make* her.'

The conversation came to an end.

When they turned into their road, five minutes later, they got a surprise. A familiar figure was standing at the Townsends' garden gate, round-shouldered and ill at ease.

CHAPTER TWELVE

Sara Does as She's Told

'Look, Davy!' said Sara, her cheeks going red.

'Evelyn Legg!' He was as surprised as Sara. 'So it is. Talk of the devil!'

Hastily the two friends braked and dismounted, pulling their bikes up on to the pavement. Like a pair of conspirators they stood in the shadow of the big horse chestnut tree at the top of the road, lest that figure in the distance should turn round and catch sight of them.

'What's she doing in our street?' muttered Davy. 'Standing outside your garden gate like that. You weren't expecting her, were you?'

'Of course not!' exclaimed Sara, completely nonplussed. 'I didn't know she even knew where I lived! How on earth did she find out?'

'Well that's easy enough,' laughed Davy. 'You're the only Townsend in the phone book, for a start. Wonder why she's turned up to see you like this – in the middle of a quiet Sunday?'

'Goodness knows.' Sara shook her head. As she got over the surprise, she gazed down the road towards the spindly figure at the garden gate. The tall girl looked nervous and hesitant, as though trying to make up her mind to go in. It was a sight that touched Sara, caught her off her guard. A feeling of optimism began to stir faintly within her. 'Perhaps . . .'

Her voice trailed away. She had been about to say *'Perhaps she does care about my friendship after all?'* But she didn't want Davy to think she was sentimental.

He finished the sentence in his own down-to-earth way.

'Perhaps she's got a conscience? Come to apologize? Could be.'

He touched Sara on the arm.

'Look, Titch, I don't want to get involved with Leggy – I'll slip off home round the back way and leave you to tackle her alone. But remember – this is your big chance, and you've got to take it.'

'You mean—' Sara looked unhappy. She stared at that distant, lonely figure. 'Force Leggy to be my racing partner?'

'It'll do her good to think about something more important than herself for a change,' said Davy, with conviction. 'If she's the wonder swimmer you say she is then she's like manna from heaven! She can't enter the big swim herself – she's burned her boats, letting you forge that note. But she can darned well help *you* win it.'

'I – I—' Sara felt confused.

'Do you want to see Kate Munro win the Cup two years running?' asked Davy.

'Oh, no – *no*!'

Sara thought very hard.

'I don't want to see the Cup go to her or to Ladymount School,' she said at last. 'Oh, Davy, I want to win it for you – I want to pay her back. And for the school, too, let's be honest. Tommy's worked so hard for something like this. I must admit I daydream about it.'

Davy nodded. Anita Thomas was one of the best-qualified PE teachers in the country and it was common knowledge she had turned down posts at older, more famous schools to come to a big, new, raw school like Hocking which had yet to build up its traditions.

'Well, girl, stop daydreaming,' Davy told Sara. 'Get on with the action! You tell Leggy to give you some races – in secret. Promise?'

'Okay.' Sara swallowed hard. 'I – I promise, Davy.'

He scooted along the pavement on his bike and turned down the narrow alley that led round to the backs of the houses. Sara watched him go and then, calmly, she mounted her cycle and rode along the road towards her house.

Leggy was walking down the Townsends' garden path now and two small boys, who had been kicking a ball in the road, shouted after her: 'Four eyes!'

'Clear off, Jason Roberts,' said Sara lightly, and the boys ran away. Leggy heard that familiar voice behind her and turned, before her finger had touched the doorbell.

'Sara!'

'Hello, Leggy,' She tried to look as casual as possible as she propped her bike up inside the front garden and joined her by the front door. 'This *is* a surprise.'

'Please don't think I've got an awful cheek.' The tall girl was clenching and unclenching her hands nervously. 'I looked you up in the phone book. I just had to come and see you.'

Sara propelled her round to the side gate.

'Come and sit in the back garden, it's nice and sunny.'

Leggy seemed relieved not to have to go into the house and meet people. There were a couple of canvas chairs on the back lawn and the two girls sank into them, facing one another. The scent of roses wafted across the shaven green lawn. Secretly, Sara felt rather pleased that their small trim garden was looking at its very best just now.

'It – it's nice to sit down,' said Leggy, finding her voice with difficulty. 'You've no idea how long I've been standing by your front gate, wondering whether to come in or not. I feel badly about yesterday.'

'I'm afraid I lost my temper,' said Sara.

'You had every right to. I've come to say sorry. You

must think I'm crazy. The downright lies I told you – about not being able to swim, being scared of water. And you being a sport like that, getting me out of swimming lessons . . .'

Leggy, who found it difficult to talk to people, had spoken disjointedly. She lapsed into silence, exhausted by the effort.

Her mouth a little dry, Sara replied.

'I could forgive all that, Leggy, if there were a good reason for it. It's the fact that you just can't be *bothered* to join in things that gets me. That you think our school's a dump and–' Sara had to swallow before she could finish the sentence. 'And – you think it's not worth your while swimming at Hocking because none of us is good enough.'

'Do you really believe that?' asked Leggy, staring at Sara. 'You really think I'm stuck up – the things you said yesterday?'

'It's what everyone else believes,' said Sara. Then, slowly; 'Leggy I *never* believed that about you before. I liked you from the minute I got to know you, and I didn't care what anyone else thought of you. Then yesterday – it all came crashing about my ears. I felt you'd let me down. That the others were right and I didn't know you properly after all. You see, I *heard* you tell your twin . . .'

'But I wasn't telling Vivienne the truth,' said Leggy simply. 'I was just putting on an act with her. I've got my pride, you see, I don't like being at Hocking. I don't want to join in things. But not because there's anything wrong with the school. I'm sure it's a great school . . .'

'Then what?'

'Oh, Sara. I'm so miserable. I feel as though I want to die.'

The tears started to stream down Leggy's cheeks and she covered her face with her hands, in shame. Sara moved her chair closer and put an arm round the tall girl's shoulders.

'Oh, Leggy. You mean – you just want *out*. Because—'

'Yes,' sobbed Leggy. The truth was coming. At last the tall girl was dropping her defences with Sara and there would be no more secrets between them. 'I hate Mummy and Daddy – I hate them! Viv and I have never been separated before. She's everything in the world to me – I don't feel as though I exist when she's not there. We've always gone to the same school – always. We started at Southdene together, last year. It was fantastic.'

'And then?'

Leggy pushed up her spectacles and smeared away the tears with the back of her hand.

'Then – without any warning, our parents told me at the end of last term that I wouldn't be going back to Southdene. Viv would be staying on but I wouldn't. They were moving here to Hocking and I would start the new term at Hocking School.'

'You mean – the fees were too much?' asked Sara. 'That wasn't fair.'

'No, no, you don't understand.' Leggy shook her head. 'Daddy's got plenty of money. It was all quite deliberate. They thought Viv and I should be split up now. That I was too dependent on her, and if I could come to a new school and stand on my own two feet I'd be better for it.'

There was silence until at last Sara found her voice. She spoke softly.

'Perhaps your parents are right, Leggy. Perhaps you will be better for it, in the long run.'

Leggy stared in shock, as though she had been slapped in the face.

'Better for being split up from Viv? Separated from my own twin sister? You're being as silly as Mummy and Daddy now, Sara. Of course I won't.' Now that she had stopped crying there was an angry, determined glint in her eye. 'What's more they'll soon find out their mistake. When it finally impinges on them how miserable I am here, and how badly my school work's going and how I haven't made any friends – when they see my report. They'll *have* to admit they're wrong and send me back to Southdene with Viv.'

Sara dropped her arm. The part about not making any friends had stung.

'I see. If you're determined that things won't work out at Hocking, then of course they won't,' she said. 'If you're just trying to prove . . .'

'No, Sara, I'm not trying to prove anything. I really am miserable. I can't help myself – honestly. I know it won't work. Do you think I wouldn't like to be happy here?'

The two girls sat in silence, and Sara chewed a piece of grass, deep in thought. She was remembering her solemn promise to Davy of half an hour ago. She was remembering too, his practical, masculine observation: *It'll do her good to think about something more important than herself for a change.*

Behind these thoughts lurked others, half-formed, mysterious.

The kitchen door opened and Mrs Townsend looked out.

'Would you and your friend like a pot of tea, Sara?' she called.

'Thanks, Mum,' replied Sara. 'We'll have it in the garden.'

She got to her feet and paced backwards and forwards across the lawn a few times. Leggy sat slumped in the blue canvas chair, watching her, drained by the outpouring of her most private emotions. She looked sad.

'It's good to know the truth at last, Leggy,' said Sara. Her manner was deliberately off-hand. 'I know what your real feelings are now, and of course I understand. It's better to know where our friendship stands, too – and that it's just going to be a temporary thing while you're here this term.'

'You're not taking things personally any more?' asked Leggy with directness.

'Of course not,' said Sara. 'But I've got a problem, too – and the thing is I need your help rather badly. You see, I've made up my mind to win the Jane Cup for Hocking School. That means beating Kate Munro. We both know that Kate can do the distance in sixty-three seconds and I'm not that fast – yet.'

'How can I help?'

'I want you to be my racing partner. I want practice races every day.'

'Oh, Sara.' Leggy passed a hand across her forehead. 'I haven't the strength really. I feel much too down in the dumps. I just don't want to get involved. Please understand.' Then her tone changed to one of relief. 'Besides – how can I? Everyone thinks I can't swim – that I'm not allowed.'

'I've got it all worked out,' said Sara coolly. 'We can sneak back and use the school pool in the evenings. No-one need ever know. You must help me.'

'No, Sara,' Leggy shrank back, panic-stricken at being drawn into Sara's problems in this way. 'I really can't. I just want to go home after school. I don't want to have to spend a minute longer there than I have to.'

'That's too bad,' said Sara, and took a deep breath. 'Then I shall have to tell Tommy about the forged note – and you'll have to swim whether you want to or not.'

'You wouldn't!' gasped Leggy. 'That's blackmail.'

'That's right,' said Sara.

CHAPTER THIRTEEN

Lesson Number One and...

'Blackmail,' repeated Leggy. The eyes were very wide open behind the spectacles. The shock had momentarily shaken her out of her self-pity. It was as though someone had stuck a pin in her. 'You're much tougher than I ever imagined. My word. *You* must want to win the big swim pretty badly.'

'I do,' said Sara. 'And I haven't a hope unless I can practise against you every day. No-one else at Hocking School is in the same class as Kate Munro – including me, at the moment. But you're her standard.'

'Oh, I know her all right.' Leggy's face registered disdain. For a few seconds she looked as though she cared about something. 'I raced against her once two years ago. She crowded me at the last turn, and got away with it.'

'She beat you?' Sara's voice had a definite edge to it. 'Then here's your chance to get your revenge, Leggy,' she said. 'Through me. What do you say?'

'I haven't much choice,' have I?' Leggy looked apathetic again. 'I don't want to get involved with *anything* at Hocking School – not even with helping you, Sara. But if it means so much to you, if you're prepared to go to such lengths to *force* me ... Well, I'll have to say yes, won't I?'

Sara was surprised that she had been able to go through with it. She had found the whole conversation distasteful. Only her promise to Davy, and the formless hope at the back of her mind, had enabled her to act out the scene.

It was with relief that at that moment she heard the sound of tea-cups rattling on a tray.

'Here's your pot of tea, Sara,' said Mrs Townsend, coming into the back garden. 'And I thought you and your friend might like some chocolate digestive biscuits.'

Sara got up from the blue canvas chair and pulled it over to the sawn-off log which they used as a garden table. She helped her mother put the tray down on top of the log, and noticed that the pink and white cups and saucers looked almost transparent in the bright light. There were two teaspoons, matching milk jug and sugar-bowl and her favourite olive-green earthenware teapot.

'Thanks, Mum,' she said. Shyly she indicated Leggy, flopped back in the garden chair, deeply withdrawn and gloomy. 'This is a friend from school, Evelyn.'

Leggy got to her feet, looking agitated.

'How do you do, Mrs Townsend,' she said, stiffly.

'Pleased to meet you.'

'Please don't think me rude, Sara, but—' Leggy turned away, 'I won't stay. I've got to get back home now – I really have.'

With that, she smoothed down her skirt and hurried across to the gate.

'Leggy—'

'It's all right, I'll see myself out.'

She glanced back in despair, as though the prospect of sipping tea on the lawn with Sara and her plump, friendly mother was too much of an ordeal. Tears were starting into her eyes again.

'Please excuse me. Good-bye.'

The gate clicked, her footsteps echoed round the side of the house and out through the front garden, and then faded into the distance. In a neighbour's garden, a motor mower started up.

'She looks a funny one,' said Mrs Townsend, put out.

'Yes,' said Sara.

She had finished pouring the tea when the side gate clicked open and Davy came tiptoeing into the back garden, grinning all over his face.

'Hello, Mrs T. Hello, Sara.'

'Just in time for a cup of tea, Davy Crockett,' said Sara's mother, brightening.

Davy sank into the canvas chair, still warm from the previous occupant. As soon as Mrs Townsend had gone indoors he looked at Sara eagerly:

'How did it go?'

'It's all fixed up,' said Sara flatly. 'I hope it's going to work.'

'Of course it's going to work. She's just the racing partner you need.'

Sara said nothing.

It was Monday the next day, and school. A fourth girl came on to the swimming scene.

'Come on, Tricia. Slant the arm downwards from the elbow to the fingertips – then pull strongly. Good girl, Hilda, you're going well today – let's see if you can break through sixty-eight seconds! Hurry up, Sara, the others are catching up on you – keep moving those legs, that's right, keep them up!'

It was a cool afternoon, but a swimming lesson was in progress. Tommy had cleared the pool for five minutes to enable the four of them to have a practice run over 100 metres.

Sara, Jane and Hilda had been joined in the water by Tricia Hope whose improvement during the past few days had been noticed and had brought her in with a chance.

'Oh, that was a lovely turn, Tricia – lovely!' shouted Tommy. 'Now accelerate – that's it – two lengths still to go, try and overtake them!'

The tanned PE teacher, in black shorts today and a white denim shirt, hopped at the side of the pool, stop-watch in hand, shouting encouragement to each of the four girls in turn. The practice race was watched by little clusters of girls on benches, shivering in their swim-suits.

'Th-they're all improving madly,' said Janice James, her teeth chattering. 'Especially Sara. Look how evenly her legs are going. Three to one on Sara to win the Heat and go through for the School in the big swim.'

'I don't know,' said Tracey Smart, who was argumentative by nature. 'Just look at Hilda. She's only just behind Sara. Her Dad's been taking her to the Baths every evening.'

'I wish they'd get on with it,' said another girl. 'I want to get back in the water – I'm freezing. As if *anyone* from Hocking School can win the Jane Cup – we all know Kate Munro is going to get it again this year.'

'Shut up!' came a chorus of furious voices.

'Right, girls!' shouted Tommy, slightly hoarse. 'You're on the last length now – and your times are splendid, all of you; now come on – pull! Bring out everything you've got.'

Blinking the water out of her eyes, Sara saw the end of the pool ahead of her. She started to speed up her arm action for the final straight. One-two-three-four-five-six, six kicks to every stroke cycle. And she must keep her legs straight – she must! She was churning up the water now, but she knew that Hilda was just behind, hanging on like a limpet.

Her chest was heaving as though it would explode, but

there was the edge – there it was! She flung out her right arm and her fingertips touched home, at least a second ahead of Hilda.

'Well done, Sara! Well done!' cried Tommy. 'Sixty-six seconds exactly – you've never done that before. And Hilda—!'

As the girls held the rail at the side of the pool recovering, Tommy went down on one knee and clapped Hilda on the shoulder.

'You're around sixty-seven seconds. Congratulations.'

As the four girls lifted themselves out of the pool, the rest of the class leapt in with shouts and whoops, swimming and splashing around. Sara and the others made for the cubicles and towelled themselves down, pleased to get their breath back. Tommy came round and spoke to each of them in turn. She reached Sara last, just as she was emerging from her cubicle.

'Well done, Sara.' Her smile was very warm indeed. 'It's exactly one week today until the Heat – and you can see that the other three are determined to give you a run for your money!'

'I'm not taking anything for granted,' said Sara.

'Good girl.' But the look in Tommy's eyes as she gazed at Sara gave her true feelings away.

'You know you're very nearly in Kate Munro's class now – don't you? I've been watching your leg action. The improvement is quite startling. Have you really done it quite of your own accord?'

Sara looked across to the wooden bench a few feet away, where Leggy was sitting within earshot. Leggy was, as usual, fully dressed and was reading a book, the 'invalid' of the class who was excused swimming lessons.

'It – it was just some advice I was given,' she said quickly.

'I wish I had more time to give you – to give all four of

you,' said Tommy, a little sadly. 'I would like to devote the whole of this week to prepare for Monday's Heat. But there's so much general PE and games to supervise. Never mind. I'll give you all the time I can.'

She walked away and Sara caught Leggy's eye and smiled. In spite of everything that had passed between them, the tall girl smiled back. Much as she wanted to remain aloof and withdrawn from it all, the fact was that Sara had just clocked her best time ever.

Soon it was evening.

Silently they climbed over the wooden fence that surrounded the school swimming pool and dropped down on to the paved terrace. Leggy and Sara, with their bathing suits wrapped in towels – and Davy, armed with a borrowed stop-watch. How silent and deserted the pool seemed in contrast to the noise and babble of the afternoon's lesson. A cool breeze ruffled the still, grey water of the pool from time to time and the only sound came from the chirping of a couple of sparrows that were surveying them from the top of the fence.

The trio had sneaked into the school through the side gate, thankful that the caretaker's bungalow lay on the far side of the grounds from the swimming pool.

'Well, here we are,' said Davy. 'You've got it all to yourselves.'

The two girls changed in adjoining cubicles and emerged shivering.

'Let's warm up,' said Leggy. Now she was in her swimsuit Sara was reminded that the apparently skinny, frail figure was in fact sinewy with muscle and there was an impression of hidden power in those rounded shoulders.

In spite of herself, Leggy looked more alive than usual. It gave her secret pleasure to be breaking school rules in this way. If nothing else, Sara's plan gave her the chance to act the rebel, defying all the mighty authority of Hocking School.

'Seeing you've forced me into this, Sara,' she said, with just a hint of good humour, 'I'm going to work you to death – you'll see!'

'Good!' said Sara, lightly. 'It's the only hope I've got.'

'You're now exactly three seconds outside Kate Munro's record for the 100 metres,' she said thoughtfully. 'I'm going to have you equalling it by the weekend, in time for the Heat on Monday.'

'And what about the big swim itself – next Thursday?'

'By that time I shall expect you to be faster than Kate Munro.'

She ran lightly over to the diving board, sprang twice and did a perfect somersault into the deep end. Davy and Sara both caught their breath and exchanged glances. It was amazing to see that tall, gawky body suddenly transformed and graceful. Sara followed and contented herself with a neat racing dive, gliding half a metre below the water.

'Just one thing,' said Leggy, as Sara surfaced. 'Lesson Number One, if you like. I think you could pick up a fraction of a second on your turns. I noticed this afternoon. Watch.'

Leggy swam easily to the end of the pool and then, in slow-motion, did a perfect imitation of Sara's turn and came swimming back to the other side.

'Is that how I turn, with a long glide underwater like that?' asked Sara.

''Fraid so,' said Leggy. 'And you lose momentum. Your glide should be shorter. Come over here and practise.'

Skilfully the tall girl coached Sara until her glide was much shorter – and her turn faster. Then they rested for five minutes, wrapped in towels.

'Okay?' asked Davy, coming up with the stop-watch. He had been watching events with interest, but was now glancing up towards the sinking sun. 'Lesson Number One's over – hadn't we better get on with a race?'

The girls glanced at one another, nodded and discarded their towels.

They took up their positions at the edge of the pool, bodies all keyed up. Davy looked down at the watch.

'Ready, steady . . .'

Sara drew in a deep breath.

CHAPTER FOURTEEN

. . . Lesson Number Two

'Go!' said Davy.

The girls made a fast start, with low racing dives, and surfaced in unison.

As she forged through the water, abreast of Leggy, friendship was forgotten for Sara. Nothing mattered but the race. This was the first time they had ever raced together. For the other girl, it was just some swimming practice, a favour she had been forced into. To Sara, it meant much, much more. She could not have explained, even to herself, why this race was so important. She only knew that she must win.

On the first length she let Leggy draw slightly ahead, using her as a pacemaker. She remembered everything that Tommy had taught her, her fingers entering first with no splash, the strong arm pull coming under the body each time, the action smooth and continuous. 'Think of swimming downhill,' the PE teacher always told the girls.

Up to the first turn – and she made it a perfect one, correcting the length of the glide. As she shot forward for the second length, she felt elated, convinced she had gained tenths of a second with her improved turn.

On and on the girls ploughed – two lengths, three lengths – and all the time Sara kept close behind Leggy, satisfied to let her make the running, and convinced that she had something in reserve for the final straight.

If she had looked up she would have seen that Davy, standing at the end of the pool, was staring at the stop-watch with some excitement. But she only saw a dark silhouette against the reddening sky, felt the surge of the water beneath her limbs, and heard the loud beat of her pounding heart.

She went down for the final turn and broke water at the same time as Leggy.

'We're dead level for the last length,' she thought. 'Now for it.'

She started to speed up her arm action, paddling straight-legged at a furious speed to give her body extra balance and propulsion. It seemed a faster pace than she had ever achieved before. As she overtook Leggy she caught a glimpse of the girl's startled face. A moment later Leggy's expression changed to one of competitive ferocity.

She forgot her apathy and her refusal to involve herself with anything connected with Hocking School. Once, when she had been happy, before she had been parted from her twin sister, she had been a champion – with all the formidable determination to win that marks the true champion. Now, briefly, the old Leggy asserted herself. This was no longer just a practice run, a favour she was being forced to do for Sara Townsend. It was a fight – and a fight that Evelyn Legg wanted to win!

Sara, on the crest of her confidence, turned her head to the right as she heard the thrashing of water alongside her.

'She's holding me,' she thought. 'She's not letting me go ahead—'

They were half-way up the final length and Sara drove herself through the water in a frenzy of speed – she mustn't let Leggy pass her, she mustn't!

They were absolutely level.

For two long seconds they fought it out, battling for supremacy. Sara felt as though her lungs would burst. Everything was starting to blur around her.

'Come on, Sara! Come on, Leggy!' Davy's excited voice came as though from a long way off, echoing around the deserted swimming pool. 'This is fantastic!'

Then easily, Leggy started to pull ahead. Sara saw the long lean streak of a body out of the corner of her eye, edging past her in the water. She thrashed away at the water helplessly in a last attempt to hold Leggy, but it was useless. It was as though she were running on the spot while her rival moved onwards.

'You're home, Leggy,' cried Davy, as she touched the side, and there was genuine admiration in his voice. 'Great swimming.'

But his real excitement was for Sara.

She touched home behind Leggy and collapsed against the side of the bath, fighting to get her breath back, her shoulders heaving.

'You'll never believe it, Titch!' He leant down, grabbing her shoulder – waving the stop-watch in his other hand. 'You'll never believe your time.'

Leggy got out of the water and peered over Davy's shoulder.

'Wheeeee!' She looked really pleased. She bent down to give Sara a hand up. 'Have a look!'

'I – I'm all in,' gasped Sara.

She sat on the edge of the pool in a daze while Davy rubbed her shoulders briskly with a towel. He was jubilant.

'Don't you want to see the stop-watch then?'

'Okay.' Sara held out her hand. 'Let's have a look.'

She stared.

'Sixty-three point five seconds!' she said. 'It can't be! That's two-and-a-half seconds faster than the fastest I've ever done!'

'And just point five of a second outside Kate Munro's record!' shouted Davy. 'Point five of a second, Sara –

that's nothing! You've put yourself right in her class with that swim. You really can win the big swim – you really can!'

It should have been a moment of triumph for Sara. Instead she felt only the aching of her body and, something else, a bitter sense of defeat.

'What was *your* time then, Leggy? It must have been good.'

'Yes, Davy – what did I do?' asked Leggy. Her voice was quiet but Sara noted that the girl was inwardly excited.

'I didn't get it exactly, as we're concentrating on Sara,' confessed Davy. 'But it was something absolutely terrific – about sixty-two something, I'd say.'

'I can still swim then,' said Leggy under her breath.

Then she pushed any excitement to one side and became her old cool self.

'I said I'd make you work,' she stated. 'Seeing you've forced me into this.'

'You made me work all right!' agreed Sara. Her voice was subdued and she was staring at Leggy with new eyes. 'You're a dark horse, I must say. I've always taken it for granted that Kate Munro's the best Junior swimmer in the county, but not any more. You're faster than she is, you must be.'

And she trembled, thinking: 'The one-minute barrier! So few Junior swimmers've ever smashed through it in England. Could Leggy?'

'Some swim!' said Davy. He could not warm to Leggy very much and his sole concern was to see Sara take the Cup off Kate Munro. But for a moment he, too, was subdued.

He spoke in a gruff embarrassed voice.

'Pity you've burned your boats and got out of swimming with that note business,' he said. 'The Cup would probably have been yours for the taking and maybe a lot more besides.'

For a moment Sara imagined she saw a tinge of regret in Leggy's eyes.

'Oh, I wouldn't say that,' she shrugged. 'I expect my time was just a fluke today. In any case, Kate's an unknown quantity. We know she's done sixty-three – but who knows *what* she could pull out of the bag if she really had to.'

She turned to Sara and spoke anxiously.

'So don't go resting on your laurels, will you? If I've *got* to be your coach I'm going to make a proper job of it. You've got to improve on today's performance – you were still outside Kate Munro's record, after all. I shan't be satisfied until you're well *inside* her time. Then – and only then – can we start getting excited about the Jane Cup. Agreed?'

'Agreed,' said Sara dully.

'You know I never felt I could care about *anything* at Hocking School,' said Leggy, suddenly. 'But I do care about this. If you can snatch the cup from Kate, then – like you said – I'd feel I was getting my revenge on her for the time she beat me. There's nothing like settling old scores.'

'Good for you, Leggy,' said Davy approvingly.

And when he and Sara cycled home together he confided:

'You know, I didn't dislike her so much this evening. You're right, she's nowhere near as high-and-mighty as she seems. In fact, I'm chuffed the way my plan is turning out – us making her help you like this. She's got an interest now – it could be the making of her.'

'Yes, I suppose it could be,' murmured Sara. Her thoughts were far away.

'And she's right – from now on you've got to get better and better.'

Sara said nothing. The bitter taste of her defeat at Leggy's hands was still with her. For of one thing she was certain. No matter how hard she tried, even if her very life depended on it, she could never this summer swim faster than she had swum this evening.

As far as she was concerned, 63.5 seconds was her limit.

'And that,' thought Sara, her pillow wet with tears that night, 'was what I would call Lesson Number Two.'

The events of the days that followed confirmed her forebodings of Monday evening.

Of course, her swimming had dramatically improved, of that there could be no doubt. The first to notice it was Hilda.

'You're beginning to leave the rest of us standing, Sara,' she said wistfully, at the end of PE on Thursday afternoon. 'What's the betting you're the one to go through for the school?'

'None of that defeatist talk, Hilda,' said Tommy sharply, overhearing. 'It's four days until the Heat – and any one of you could hit peak form between now and then.'

Anita Thomas believed in stimulating the competitive spirit amongst the girls, but she was not the best actress in the world. Her hopes of bringing the coveted trophy home to Hocking, a school that was so young and so badly in need of its first big win at *something*, were firmly pinned on Sara. Everyone could see that now.

That made the secret training sessions with Leggy and Davy all the more painful for Sara. Every evening that week they had repeated Monday's drill – meeting like conspirators at the school pool, after everyone had gone home.

The idea of turning Sara into a champion had now captured Leggy's imagination. She became absorbed in the task, even though nothing else at Hocking School absorbed her. She lent Sara books on swimming, full of diagrams, determined to get her crawl technically perfect. Every evening she found there was something new to teach and her pupil was eager to learn.

Yet as each day passed, Sara became more despondent. She simply could not surpass the time she had achieved on Monday – 63.5 seconds. That time, which had seemed nothing short of a miracle at first, became odious to her. Only once more, by a lung-bursting onslaught, did she manage to get near it – and most of the time she fell considerably short of it.

'So much for me getting better and better!' she said on Friday evening. 'I just get worse – and worse – and *worse.*'

She was close to tears. It was the end of the school week. She and Leggy had just swum a poor race, which had begun with two false starts, and Davy's face as he announced the finishing time was doleful.

' 'Fraid it's not so hot tonight, Titch. Sixty-six point nine seconds.'

'It's hopeless,' said Sara. She felt angry and disheartened. 'I can't even equal Kate Munro's present record – let alone what she might produce in the big swim.'

'I've had an idea,' said Leggy quietly. More than once this week, Sara had sensed the tall girl getting impatient with her, but managing to hide it. Now there was only sympathy in her eyes. 'It's Saturday tomorrow – let's give training a rest. Let's go and watch some swimming instead.'

'Watch what?'

'I've found out that Ladymount School's got a home

swimming match – against St Bede's. Starring Kate Munro, of course. There's nothing to stop us going as spectators.'

'You think that will spur me on? Seeing her in action. I tell you – it'll only depress me more.'

'I feel guilty,' said Leggy. 'I know I've been laying it on thick about Kate – but I found something out this morning. Apparently she's been right off form for the past few days. Perhaps I've been making her too much of a bogeyman. Let's go and see her, anyway. It's always a good thing to keep a close eye on the competition.'

'Hmm.' Sara's ill humour began to leave her. 'You mean it might cheer me up – if she swims badly? What do you feel like, Davy?'

'I'd love to come and boo Kate Munro,' said Davy. 'But not on a Saturday afternoon – I'm playing cricket.'

The tall girl looked so disappointed that Sara said on impulse:

'Okay, Leggy. I'll go, if you think it's a good idea.'

CHAPTER FIFTEEN

Kate Munro Wins, Again

The two girls met at the cross-roads after lunch on Saturday.

Leggy was there first, standing with her bicycle. She looked relieved when Sara came pedalling round the corner of Station Road.

'Sorry I'm late, Leggy – I had to help Mum with the washing-up.'

'I thought you'd ducked out.'

Sara smiled. It was true she hadn't exactly rushed, lingering over the drying-up at home, polishing the cutlery until it shone.

'I can't say I'm dying to see Kate Munro in action,' she said, as the girls set off on their bikes. 'I'm a coward.'

'It'll do nothing but good,' said Leggy firmly. 'You've got a hang-up about her. You think she's invincible – and I'm to blame as much as anyone. I was hoping to spur you on, but I've sapped your confidence instead.'

Sara wanted to tell Leggy that it had nothing to do with her confidence. She simply felt it to be a fact that she would not this season improve upon that lung-bursting swim of 100 metres in 63.5 seconds last Monday, Kate or no Kate. But it was a difficult thing to confess to Leggy, who was putting so much into coaching her. After all, Leggy had found an interest in life at last; she was not nearly so moody at school. She was obviously pining less for Vivienne. It would be a shame to spoil it while it lasted. Instead, Sara said:

'I hope you're right, Leggy. I hope she really is off form.'

'So I've heard.'

'If she is – and if she *stays* off form – then—' Sara began to hope, just a little, 'I'm in with a chance!'

Sara was not acting now. In her more optimistic moods she still dreamt of defeating the champion.

'Look – quite a crowd's turned up!' she said as they turned in through the gates of Ladymount School. On a big area of tarmac outside the school buildings, at the end of the swerving gravelled drive, dozens of cars were parked. They were in neat rows, their rooftops gleaming in the sunshine, blue and grey and silver.

Beyond the cars was a dusty red coach which had transported the swimming team and its supporters from St Bede's.

The friends crunched up the drive and then parked their bikes. In silence they walked to a large white building on the far side of the grounds. They went along flagged mossy pathways, across lawns as smooth as green velvet, past flower beds that hummed with bees and shimmered with colour and perfume. For the main building of Ladymount School had been a gentleman's residence in the eighteenth century and the grounds were still cared for by its gardeners as meticulously now as two hundred years ago.

In contrast the white block that housed Ladymount's indoor swimming pool was extremely modern; it had been *avant garde* when it had been built ten years ago and with its sloping walls and flat roof was still distinctly contemporary. Through the high slit windows came the sound of muffled cheers. The swimming match had started.

'I suppose it's all right for us to go in?'

'Of course it is,' said Leggy. 'These inter-school

matches are always open to the public. Besides, who'll notice us among so many?'

She was wrong there.

At first sight it looked as though every seat was taken inside the crowded pool. Then they noticed a couple of places at the end of a bench quite near the changing cubicles. They squeezed on the end and Sara gazed about her. The pool was heated and the atmosphere was damp and warm, with that special tang of chlorine in the air. The spectators were buzzing with excitement for St Bede's had just snatched a six-point lead in the 100 metres Senior breast-stroke. The pool was still and green; it looked inviting.

'Lucky things,' she whispered. 'They swim here all year round.'

It was not surprising that Ladymount had produced a string of outstanding swimmers in the past few years, of whom Kate Munro was the latest in the line.

'Ssssh,' said Leggy, completely absorbed now. 'It's the diving next.'

The diving events were close and thrilling, and then came the Senior 4 × 100 metres relay race, with St Bede's best Senior swimmer, Marge Matthews, snatching a breath-taking win from Ladymount's Gloria Smith in the final leg.

There was a short interval and conversation was humming all around them.

'Neck and neck.'

'Only the Junior swimming events to go.'

'Don't worry—' said a Ladymount voice, with the mixture of pride and hero-worship that Sara had noticed before. 'They've no-one to touch Kate. Kate'll thrash 'em alive.'

Even as Sara remembered, with a butterfly feeling in her stomach, their purpose in coming to watch this match, someone stepped out of the changing cubicle just a few feet away from them.

Several heads turned. It was Kate Munro, lithe and strong with a beautiful tan, looking stunning in a regulation red and white Ladymount swimming costume. She was casually tucking her long red hair into a bathing cap, taking her time as she walked.

'Good luck, Kate!' someone hissed.

'You show 'em.'

Right alongside Sara and Leggy, the girl stopped. She was staring not at Sara but at Leggy, and her mouth was open.

'What are you doing here?' she asked rudely.

'I – I came to watch.' Leggy was blushing, disconcerted at being recognized. 'It's a free country, isn't it?'

'But I haven't bumped into you for two years.' Now Kate Munro was looking rather disconcerted herself. 'I thought you'd moved out of the county.'

'No. I'm at Hocking Scool.'

'What!' sniggered Kate. Then, with an unkind twist to her mouth: 'What happened, did your parents run out of funds?'

'Shut up!' said Sara, softly. But Kate was staring into space, somewhere above Leggy's head, and frowning.

'I'll be meeting you in the Jane next week then—?'

'Oh, no I—'

Kate didn't even hear; she said with a frown:

'Well as you've come along to spy on my form, I'll give you a little exhibition. I've been taking it easy lately but now I feel great. The sight of you has put me right in the mood, Evelyn Legg.'

'Take your positions, please,' crackled a voice through a megaphone. 'The next race is the 4 × 50 metres Junior Relay Race, free-style. Will the teams get into position.'

Kate ran to the end of the bath and casually dived in. A

roar went up from her supporters and there was applause as she surfaced and climbed out after doing a few strokes to limber up. Then she took up her position at this end of the pool with her team-mate. The start and the finish were at the far end of the pool and there were other girls waiting down there.

'Kate's doing the final leg then,' whispered Sara.

Leggy looked agitated.

'She recognized me, Sara,' she whispered in alarm. 'Supposing the word gets round – supposing it gets back to Tommy? That I can swim . . .'

'*Used* to swim,' pointed out Sara, giving Leggy's arm a reassuring squeeze. 'You're not swimming now, are you? Kate Munro won't make any trouble. She'll be only too relieved that you're *not* going to take part in the big swim.'

As the logic of Sara's words struck Leggy, she visibly relaxed.

Then – a crack from the starting-pistol and the race had begun.

As the first two team members swam the first leg neck and neck the cheering began. The Number Twos dived into the water simultaneously but slowly the St Bede's girl drew ahead and the third leg started with Ladymount well behind.

'Come on, Daphne!' screamed the Ladymount supporters. 'Catch!'

But the St Bede's Number Three was a stronger swimmer and instead of narrowing the gap, Ladymount fell even farther behind.

'It's up to you now, Kate!' yelled a crowd of girls nearby.

'You've got to win or we'll lose the match.'

As the Number Three swimmers came up the pool towards the near end, Kate Munro moved forward to take her position at the edge. She still had a few seconds before her Number Three touched and slowly, deliberately, she turned round.

She was staring straight at Leggy with a look of arrogant determination on her face which said: 'Now you'll see something!'

Then she crouched in position for a racing start as the St Bede's Number Four flashed into the water. Panting and disheartened Ladymount's Daphne touched the side, as though the race were already lost.

'Kate!' shrieked the onlookers. 'Kate!'

Like an arrow from a bow, Kate Munro shot into the water in a beautiful racing dive. She was at least ten metres behind her rival. It looked an impossible position.

But soon the spectators realized that something sensational was happening. They leaped to their feet, shouting and screaming. 'Kate's gaining! She's gaining!' Even Sara, forgetting herself, found that she was standing up watching the breathtaking speed of Kate Munro as she ploughed through the water, gaining on her rival, metre by metre, with a crawl that would have done justice to an Olympic champion.

'Kate! KATE! KATE!'

'You can do it, love – you can do it!'

The whole building reverberated with the cheers as Kate Munro fought it out with her rival, neck and neck, only inches from the finish – and then a fantastic roar went up.

'She's done it!'

'Kate's won!'

It took some minutes for the commotion to die down. Sara sank back into her seat, feeling weak all over. Then there was silence, a breathless stillness as the timekeeper stepped forward, stop-watch in hand. She was holding a megaphone to her lips and Sara heard the crackling announcement, echoing around the pool, echoing in her head.

'Although it is not an official record and cannot be ratified, I have some very thrilling news. Kate Munro has just swum 50 metres free-style in twenty-nine seconds which beats the all-England Junior record for this year by four-tenths of a second.'

Sara sat there slumped, feeling helpless as the applause echoed and re-echoed around them. That speed sustained (could she sustain it?) over 100 metres next Thursday, and Kate Munro would be through the one-minute barrier.

Leggy's face was a picture of dismay.

A figure came sauntering their way. Kate Munro was on her way back to her changing cubicle. Sara rose to her feet and grabbed Leggy's arm.

'Come on – let's get out of here.'

Instead Leggy confronted Kate, and her voice shook a little.

'If that was for my benefit, you were wasting your time.'

'Why, think you can do better?' sneered the champion.

'I don't swim any more. Medical reasons.'

Kate stared at Leggy. She almost laughed out loud with relief.

'*Really?*'

Then, looking Leggy up and down, she frowned in disbelief.

'Medical reasons? Come off it. You're as strong as a horse. You're trying to trick me. Get me to slacken off . . .'

'Believe what you like,' said Leggy shortly, and swung round to Sara. 'This is who you'll be swimming against in the Jane Cup. Sara Townsend – not me. Come on, Sara – let's go.'

'Don't make me laugh,' said Kate as they walked away. Within seconds she was engulfed in a mob of small but ardent fans.

CHAPTER SIXTEEN

Davy's Indiscretion

Outside, Sara and Leggy made their way through the sunlit grounds in silence. Sara was feeling very, very depressed. Any dreams she had once had were completely shattered now.

There was a strange expression on Leggy's face.

'I wish I *were* swimming in the Jane Cup,' she said bitterly. To have a go at beating her.'

'So do I wish you were,' sighed Sara.

'Oh, Sara!' Leggy looked at her as they picked up their cycles. 'I'm sorry. This was the most stupid idea of mine. Now you're going to be more hung-up over Kate Munro than ever.'

'That's impossible,' said Sara. 'I've known since Monday that I haven't a hope. I'm not really in the same class.'

'Sara, we mustn't talk like this!' said Leggy suddenly. She began to be alarmed at the danger of all the hard work she had put into coaching Sara going for nought. 'We mustn't be defeatist. It's the Heat at school on Monday – you mustn't let yourself go, or we'll find Hilda or Jane representing the school before we can turn round.'

'What difference would it make?' asked Sara miserably.

'Stop talking like this!'

'What do you suggest?'

'Well – it's like falling off a horse, you have to get back on as quickly as possible.' Leggy's eyes gleamed behind her glasses. 'I've got to get you back in the water before Monday.'

'But tomorrow's Sunday. The main school gates are padlocked. We can't do our usual practice in the school pool – it's too risky.'

'Then—' Leggy stopped. They were cycling back towards the town. It was a full ten seconds before she finished her sentence. 'We'll have to go to the public swimming baths.'

'But supposing someone sees you swimming?' asked Sara, surprised and touched that Leggy should throw all caution to the winds for her sake. 'Someone from school. You're supposed to be an invalid, remember.'

'I'll just have to take a chance. If we go there early, just after breakfast, the Baths will be almost empty. You've *got* to have one more practice before the Heat.'

Sara was silent. She was thinking very hard. Finally:

'Okay. I'll come. Let's say half-past nine in the morning.'

'Good girl. You can still give Kate Munro a run for her money.'

The next morning, Sara's mother asked:

'Have you caught a cold, my girl, with all this swimming?'

'Cold, Mummy?'

'Oh, that's better. I thought your voice sounded quite odd when you were phoning – husky.'

'I have got a bit of a throat this morning,' said Sara.

'Going somewhere?'

'Yes, just fixing things up,' said Sara. 'I'm dashing off after breakfast to meet Leggy. We're going swimming at the Baths. Davy's coming too, to time us.'

'You'd better not eat anything too heavy then,' said Mrs Townsend practically. 'Why not have some cereal – and I'll cook you something when you get back.'

Sara sat in the kitchen and ate her cornflakes very slowly.

'When's this race then, dear? It must be soon now.'

'Er – yes, tomorrow,' said Sara, with her mouth full. Her thoughts were far away. 'The Heat at school, that is. The Jane Cup's not till Thursday, but tomorrow will decide which of us is going to swim for the school.'

'And you've made up your mind it's going to be you, haven't you?' said her mother. 'You deserve to, dear, all this swimming you've been doing. You must be good by now.'

'Not bad,' said Sara, non-committally. Her mother had been quite athletic as a girl. She would be proud if Sara brought the Jane Cup home to Hocking, proving herself the best Junior girl swimmer in the whole county. Even as that thought struck Sara, she felt gloomy and glanced out of the kitchen window at the sky. What a grey morning it was.

She called for Davy and they set off on their bikes. They met up with Leggy at the foot of Hocking Hill. She was waiting patiently, her towel and swimming costume bulging out of her small saddlebag.

'Come on, snails.' Her eyes were bright behind her glasses as they started up the steep hill. Before long they decided to dismount and push their cycles, taking it slowly to give them breath to talk.

'Have you told Davy about yesterday?'

'You bet she has,' said Davy. 'You were dead right to want to get Sara back in the water today, Leggy. Kate Munro might be horrible, but the girl certainly can swim.'

'I've been thinking about her time,' said Leggy cheerfully. 'It depressed us yesterday didn't it, Sara—'

'You can say that again.'

'But it *shouldn't.* Kate practically burst a blood vessel doing that time – she won't be able to pull anything like that out of the bag again for weeks, maybe not all season!'

'You mean – you think she's shot her bolt?' said Davy.

'Yes,' said Leggy. 'I know a bit about racing. No-one can keep up that sort of performance. I don't think she'll touch that speed in the big swim, you mark my words.'

Sara, pushing harder as the hill got steeper, glanced at Leggy's face. The tall girl's cheeks were a little flushed and she scarcely noticed the climb, so absorbed was she in Sara's chances for the Cup. She looked somewhat different from the sullen, silent girl who had arrived at Hocking School the week before last.

'Must have a rest,' puffed Davy, when they were well up the hill. 'You two are a couple of Amazons.'

Leggy smiled as the three of them sat down on a grassy bank at the side of the road, holding on to their bikes. It was true, she was still fresh as a daisy. How very deceptive appearances can be, thought Sara. This skinny, round-shouldered girl with spectacles was as strong and sinewy as an ox! But no-one at school could have suspected it – it had not been difficult to deceive them.

'By the way,' asked Sara casually. 'How's Vivienne these days? Aren't you seeing her this weekend?'

'She's fine,' replied Leggy comfortably. Yet not long ago, Sara knew, such a question would have thrown the twin into brooding silence. 'As a matter of fact – ' Leggy plucked a piece of grass, then sucked the stem absentmindedly ' – she's over here for the day.'

'Really?'

Sara was astonished, but tried not to show it. Leggy had left Vivienne at home, willing to miss her company for an hour while she got on with the business of coaching Sara. Unbelievable!

'This *is* progress,' she thought. She suddenly felt very pleased and wanted to turn to Leggy and say triumphantly, 'You can be happy at Hocking School, you know. You *can* exist in your own right. Whatever happens about the big swim.'

Instead she got slowly to her feet and said:

'Let's get going.'

But before the three of them could wheel their bikes back on to the road there was the sudden roar of a sports-car engine changing down through its gears as it came up Hocking Hill. The white two-seater approached slowly. Kate Munro was in the passenger seat and the driver was her swimming coach, Grundy. She told him to brake, on the hill.

'Just been to get the *Sunday Star*!' she said, waving the thick regional Sunday newspaper in their faces. 'I'm splattered all over the back page.'

'Wish you were,' said Davy.

Suddenly Kate's expression changed, and she looked put out. For a moment Sara thought that Davy's remark might possibly have impinged on her good opinion of herself. But Kate was looking straight at Leggy's swimming things, sticking out of the saddlebag on her bike.

'I thought you didn't swim – medical reasons.'

Leggy was so covered in confusion that Sara stepped in quickly.

'Why so surprised? You didn't believe it, anyway.'

'But I've made inquiries!' snapped Kate. 'I was told it really was true. Evelyn really is off games – her mother sent a letter to your Thomas person.'

'Well, actually she forged the letter so as to conserve her strength to beat you on Thursday,' said Davy sarcastically.

'In that case,' said Kate Munro, going rather white, 'she'll be expelled and serves her right. Come on, Grundy. Let's get home.'

'*Davy!*' gasped Leggy, as the car roared off. 'Whatever

made you say a stupid thing like that. Don't you realize – *she believed you*?'

'I – I was just trying to laugh the whole thing off, get rid of her,' said Davy. His face was very red. 'Oh, Leggy – I could bite my tongue off, honest.'

'She can tell Tommy! She probably *will* tell Tommy—' there was real panic in Leggy's voice. 'Just for the sheer fun of seeing me get expelled, she's that sort of girl—'

'Don't get hysterical!' Sara said suddenly, with a real edge to her voice 'You didn't forge that note, I did. So we'd both get expelled. Forget it. Kate Munro won't do anything.'

CHAPTER SEVENTEEN

Tommy Finds Out

'Come on, Titch, stop fooling about,' said Davy, who had been on edge ever since the meeting with Kate Munro. He stood by the pool in his shorts, holding his stop-watch. The two girls were in the water. After Davy's clanger, Leggy had been doubly relieved to find that, as she had hoped, Hocking Baths were almost empty at this time of a Sunday morning. There would not be more than ten other swimmers there and, to Leggy's satisfaction, none of them was known to the girls.

'Oh, but we're enjoying ourselves, Davy,' protested Sara.

They had been limbering up, diving from the high board – a luxury the school swimming pool did not possess – and seeing how far they could swim underwater. Sara had beaten Leggy every time, which had been good for her morale, and now she was idly floating on her back. She was behaving as though she had all the time in the world.

'Well, I don't want to hurry you but I've got a stack of homework to do.'

'You mean you want to go home and watch cricket on the box!' laughed Sara. 'All right then – just one more dive, *please*, Davy.'

She climbed out of the pool then lightly ran up the wooden ladders to the very top diving board. The hessian felt warm and damp beneath her feet and she had a superb view of the entire pool. She glimpsed a car pulling up outside the Swimming Baths. The car looked familiar. Then she dived.

'Great!' said Leggy as she surfaced. 'Lovely dive, Sara.'

'I'm ready for our race now,' said Sara. 'Let's get on with it.'

They took up their positions at the edge while Davy set the stop-watch. Sara was keyed up. She wanted this to be a good race.

Davy stayed at this end of the pool, for the girls were to race two lengths – exactly 100 metres.

'Go!' he shouted, and the girls dived in.

Sara broke water with a strong arm pull. She was going all out for an early burst of speed to put Leggy on her mettle. She pounded through the water, knowing that she was taking the risk of an early fade-out, but Leggy stayed with her neck and neck.

'Atta girl!' gasped Leggy as they came up for the turn at the far end of the pool. Through a blur Sara glimpsed a figure standing there. Then she went down in a forward somersault for the tumble turn, pushed off from the wall with her feet, did a short glide on her back, and then twisted to the surface to swim back down the baths. She saw the figure again out of the corner of her eye – now running to keep up with them.

On the first half of the length Sara pulled out everything she possessed, churning up the water at speed and managing, when turning her head for breath, to splutter a taunt at Leggy—

'Slow-coach!'

That did it. Leggy's face took on its ferocious look and steadily she surged forward. Sara fought every inch of the way, her lungs bursting and her head pounding, but Leggy seemed to glide through the water as though she were powered by a hidden motor.

She won, easily. Davy was excited.

'Sixty-two seconds, Leggy!' he shouted. And then – as

Sara touched home, 'Sixty-three point five! You're right back on form again, Titch!'

He was so pleased and happy that he was completely unaware of the tall figure standing just behind him. He helped first one girl out of the water and then the other. Leggy brushed the water from her eyes and stared.

Anita Thomas stared back.

'Oh!' gasped Leggy, her face as white as a sheet.

The PE teacher from Hocking School was dressed in casual clothes – blue slacks and a bright yellow shirt. A few seconds before, her eyes had been bright with interest as she watched the two girls racing, but now her tanned face was set and stony.

'Good morning, Evelyn. Good morning, Sara,' she said in a dry voice. 'So the anonymous message I received was *not* a hoax.'

'Message?' said Leggy, trembling. Then, to herself: 'Kate Munro!'

'Someone rang and told me what I would see if I came here now. I was inclined to ignore it, but my curiosity got the better of me. Well, well, well.'

Tommy turned to gaze at Sara and her look gave Sara butterflies inside. Exhausted from her swim and like Leggy trembling a little, she leant against Davy for support. It was comforting to feel him put an arm around her shoulders for a moment, protectively.

'How long have you known?'

'I – I–'

But the question was perfunctory. Tommy was not really interested in the answer. All her attention was focused on Leggy. She was very, very angry – but mingled with the anger was admiration that she could only hide with difficulty.

'That was quite some swim, Evelyn Legg. I thought you were forbidden to swim because of "medical" reasons.

You had the look to me of someone who spends a great deal of time in the water. Of a champion swimmer in fact. I have a shrewd suspicion that if I weren't new to this county I might have heard of you.' She said the word 'champion' as though it almost choked her.

'It wasn't true about the medical reasons,' said Leggy in a whisper.

'I gather that,' said Tommy. 'You look as tough as leather. You – you deceitful girl! Why did you pretend to me that you couldn't swim? Why? You obviously forged your own mother's handwriting – a disgraceful thing to do. Now I'm in a position where I have to punish you. You may even have to be suspended. There can hardly be any question of you having the honour of swimming for the school . . .'

The PE teacher's voice dropped to a whisper. She could not hide her bitter dismay.

'. . . And all the time I had a champion swimmer in my midst. A girl who can swim like a fish. Someone with a real chance of bringing the Jane Cup home to Hocking School!'

She bit her lip, suddenly realizing how much she was saying – that she must, surely, be hurting Sara's feelings.

'I'm sorry, Sara.'

Sara forgave her. She knew how much Tommy wanted to put Hocking School on the map and that winning the Cup had become almost an obsession with her. She realized as she stood there shivering beneath the grey sky that at this moment she scarcely existed for Anita Thomas.

'Leggy *can* swim for the School,' she said quietly. 'There's no reason on earth why she should be punished. It's all my fault.'

'Your fault?' exclaimed Tommy. She turned to Sara with raised eyebrows. She tried to look severe but there was no doubt that her eyes were alight with expectancy. 'What do you mean?'

'The whole thing was my idea,' said Sara. 'I talked Leggy – I mean Evelyn – into it. She wasn't keen to swim because she's self-conscious about her figure – so I thought: Why should she? I made it all so easy for her,' the confession came out with a rush. 'I was the one who forged that letter from her mother.'

'Hey, steady on—' began Leggy.

'Shut up,' said Sara, giving her an absolutely freezing stare – daring her to say another word. 'It's the truth. I did the letter. So if there's any punishment to be meted out, punish me, Tommy. But please, *please* give Leggy a chance to win the big swim.'

CHAPTER EIGHTEEN

The Swimmer is Chosen

'Is this the truth, Evelyn?' asked Tommy in astonishment. 'That it was Sara and not you who forged the note in your mother's writing?'

'I – I—' Leggy stared at Sara helplessly. 'Yes, it is true. But—'

'Don't listen to her! She never wanted to do it,' Sara began to embellish the story still further, 'I forced her into it. You see she's grown six inches since last summer. She was self-conscious about looking skinny in a bathing suit – looking like a beanpole.'

'Self-conscious about your figure – oh, you poor child.' The teacher turned to Leggy. She didn't believe it, but here was the loophole she badly wanted! Sara was making it all so easy. 'And you allowed yourself to be egged on in this deception? That was wrong, but I can't be too angry.'

'Please, I—' Once more Leggy tried to speak, her sense of honesty outraged by the performance Sara was putting on for her benefit. Then, under Sara's withering glance, she lapsed into silence.

'Why did you do it, Sara?' asked Tommy quietly.

'I felt sorry for her,' she replied. That at least was the simple truth.

'Did you realize then that she was a champion swimmer? No, surely not—'

'No, I was absolutely flabbergasted when I found out. By that time it was too late.'

'I see,' said the teacher. She was very thoughtful for a moment. 'I believe you. But to forge a letter was a very serious offence and,' she turned on Leggy, straining to be fair now 'and you could have stopped it Evelyn, however persuasive Sara was. The fact is that I know you have had very real reasons for being unhappy about starting your new school this term. I was warned that I must be prepared to make allowances. Of the two of you, Sara is the one who should have known better. I must punish you both, but Sara the more severely.'

Both girls waited for her next words, almost holding their breath. Davy, who had been looking rather stunned through all this, began to chew his thumbnail.

'I forbid you to take part in the Heat at school tomorrow, Sara,' said Tommy. 'That shall be your punishment – to lose your chance of swimming for the school. And I believe you had set your heart on it.'

'Yes, I had,' said Sara. 'And—'

'Evelyn – you are to write out one thousand times, "I must not practise deception at Hocking School", by Wednesday.'

'And she's to be allowed to enter the Heat?' asked Sara anxiously.

'Oh, certainly,' said Anita Thomas. She looked straight at Leggy and for the first time there was a hint of good humour in her eyes. 'Not only do I expect her to win the Heat tomorrow. The very least she can do, if she wants to make amends for her behaviour, is to go through and win the Jane for Hocking School. That is an order, Evelyn. Do you understand?'

With that the PE teacher turned on her heel.

'And now I am going home to weed my garden. It *is* Sunday after all.'

'Did you see her face?' whispered Davy, after she had gone. 'She's as pleased as Punch. Who'd have thought she'd have taken it so calmly.'

'Of course she has,' said Sara. 'She wants the school to

win the Cup and now—' she turned to Leggy. 'It can. You've had your orders. You're to go through and win that Cup, give Kate Munro the thrashing of her life. From *all* of us.'

'Don't worry,' said Leggy, looking angry. 'I shall – or at least I shall do my very best. I could strangle her for this.'

'For what?'

'For taking away your chance, Sara, that's what. *She* rang up Tommy and told on me – it stands out a mile. She thought it would get me expelled – or suspended! I'll make her sorry!'

'You do that.'

'I'll try. I owe it to you, Sara,' Leggy went on, calming down. 'You should never have taken all the blame like that – it was a really sporting thing to do.'

'But sensible. Making the best of a bad situation.' Davy's voice was gruff. He had worked so hard for Sara's chance, timed her practice swims, bought her coffees, given her encouragement when she had got down-hearted. He had been inspired by a vision: of his school doing something really big, and Sara doing it. Sara would never do it now, perhaps because of his own stupid tongue. That was a hard thing to face up to.

Yet for some days now Davy had felt bothered that Leggy was the better swimmer; had kept casting the thought aside. She stood a better chance of beating the champion than Sara did. Now he looked that fact squarely in the face and was prepared to put his personal feelings to one side.

'There would have been no sense in you *both* getting banned, would there, Leggy? Sara handled things just the right way.'

Once more Davy put his arm round Sara's shoulders and gave her a hug which said far more than words could.

'Come on, Titch,' he whispered. 'Time to get changed.'

The next day at school the news created a sensation.

'Come over here, mates!' guffawed Terry Horn. 'Just come and take a look at this!'

A crowd was gathered round the Sports Notice Board. The list had gone up of the girls who would be entering today's Heat.

Sara heard the laughter as she passed the end of the corridor, and she could see Terry and his friends almost doubled up with mirth.

'Leggy!'

'She's put her name down!'

'Fancies herself as a swimming champion – oh, no!'

The news flashed round the buildings. Everyone was agog. The other entrants for the race were completely bewildered.

'Why haven't you put your name down, Sara?' whispered Hilda, just before lessons started. 'You're the favourite.'

'I've been banned, that's all. Breaking school rules.' Sara would say no more.

Jane and Tricia pumped Sara mercilessly. They were sure that she knew something.

'Who put Leggy's name down? It is a joke, isn't it?'

'I shouldn't think so.'

'But she hasn't been in the water all term. She can't even swim, can she? Isn't she supposed to be some kind of invalid?'

'Isn't she supposed to have acne?'

'You mean asthma, don't you?'

'She definitely brought a note from her mother.'

'Well maybe she's better now,' smiled Sara.

'*Can* she swim then? Is she good then? Oh – she can't be, she just hasn't got the build.'

'We'll just have to wait and see, won't we?' said Sara.

'You certainly will,' said Old Noah sternly, standing just behind them. 'I am waiting to start the lesson.'

At the end of the afternoon the school swimming pool was lined with spectators. The news had got round that it wasn't a joke. The odd new girl, with her round shoulders and her spectacles, had herself put her name down for the Heat and with Tommy's full approval. It was astonishing.

Terry Horn and his gang turned up for the entertainment. They had even rigged up a banner: 'Leggy for Champion' and it caused a ripple of amusement to run around the pool.

'Silence, please!' said Anita Thomas angrily, striding down the length of the pool, her PE whistle in her hand. 'The race will start in four minutes.'

Leggy emerged from the changing cubicle in her dark swimming suit, without her spectacles. Her cheeks were the colour of beetroot.

'Think she'll be able to see where she's going?' laughed someone.

Leggy heard, and trembled. Her courage almost deserted her. She looked as though she were about to turn and run away.

Suddenly, Sara was at her side, squeezing her arm.

'You show them,' she said softly.

'Okay.' Leggy's courage came back. 'I owe it to you, Sara.'

'Wheeeee!' went the whistle, and the race started.

The school pool rang with cheers as Jane, Hilda, Tricia and Leggy fought it out for the first length.

Then slowly, very slowly, the cheers died away. There was an uneasy silence.

After the first turn, the other three simply weren't in the race. Effortlessly Leggy forged ahead, leaving them far behind. Arms flailing, chests heaving, the others tried to catch up. Leggy simply increased her lead, metre by metre. As she came down the finishing straight, Sara and Davy broke the silence as they shouted in unison:

'Three cheers for Leggy!'

Only then did it fully dawn on the stunned spectators that they had a champion in their midst; that what they were watching was not only in their imaginations – it was all really happening.

'Hurray!'

The cheers started in a small way and then built up to a crescendo of screams as Leggy touched home, half a length ahead of Hilda.

'Leggy – Leggy – LEGGY!'

They swarmed about her as she climbed out of the water, patting her on the back, elated for Hocking School.

In all the excitement the other three contestants were forgotten. In the short space of one minute and one-and-a-half seconds Leggy had been transformed from a nonentity into a heroine.

CHAPTER NINETEEN

The Big Swim of the Summer

On Thursday, two coaches left Hocking School for Bardsley. Tommy had only planned to hire a minibus, to take the school's entrant for the Jane Cup with a few supporters. But such was the excitement and interest that now the two enormous silver coaches were packed with supporters, determined to cheer Leggy to victory.

Leggy sat in the back of the first coach, between Sara and Davy.

'Well, this is it,' said Davy. 'Face to face with Kate Munro.'

'I'm going to show her,' said Leggy. 'I've never forgiven her for ringing up Tommy.'

'Not to mention the time her dog ate my trousers,' said Davy, just to give her extra incentive. 'I want revenge for that, remember.'

'I won't forget,' she said. She was keyed up with nervous tension. 'But she's good – very good. The local papers take it for granted this morning that she's going to win the big swim for the second year. The only question is what time she'll do.'

'Then the papers are in for a surprise, aren't they?' said Sara softly. Then, changing the subject: 'Is Vivienne getting over?'

'She hopes to,' said Leggy, happily. 'She's trying to get a lift up.'

The noise at Bardsley Swimming Baths was deafening. The eight best girl swimmers from schools all over the area were taking part in the Cup Race and coach loads of supporters had come for miles to cheer. Dotted all around could be seen the pink-and-grey striped blazers of Ladymount School.

'It looks as though the whole school's come to cheer Kate Munro,' said Sara to Davy as they took up their seats.

'Well, our lot will make more noise,' he laughed. 'Girls are too ladylike to really bellow.'

'Don't you believe it,' said Sara. 'You should have heard them when Kate did twenty-nine seconds against St Bede's.'

What a time! Tommy, who was just about to sit down in the seat next to them, gave a little shudder.

'Do you think Evelyn can beat the Munro girl, Sara?' she asked. She was very pale, more nervous even than Leggy herself. Suddenly she was desperately uncertain. 'Do you think she *can*?'

'If anyone can, she can,' said Sara.

An expectant hush descended over the pool as the eight competitors came out of their changing cubicles. All of them wore different colours, the regulation bathing suits of their respective schools. One by one they plunged into the water to limber up. Madge Daltry from Bardsley High looked magnificent in white. She had a model's figure and a crowd of local boys whistled. Conversation broke out again for a few minutes and then an announcement came crackling over the loudspeakers.

'Will contestants for the Jane Cup Race please get into position.'

Once more, silence. As the girls formed a neat line at one end of the baths the only movement came from two press photographers taking up their positions, cameras at the ready.

Leggy stood erect, very still. Now that the great moment had come she was calm, with the control over her temperament that every true competitor must have. She did not even glance at Kate Munro, who stood at the end of the line in lane No. 8.

Nor did the conceited girl show any trace of nerves. Some of her thick red hair had fallen out of her bathing cap and with studied nonchalance she tucked it in, moments before the race was due to start.

One of her supporters darted forward from the crowd and patted her on the back. And then a girl in a pink-and-grey blazer yelled:

'Give the bean pole a thrashing, Kate!'

Kate turned and looked at Leggy and made the 'thumbs-down' sign and a roar of approval went up from the Ladymount supporters.

'Silence, please!' crackled the loudspeakers. 'The race will be swum over 100 metres – two lengths of this pool. Silence, please!'

Sara glanced at Davy, crossed her fingers and held her breath.

Eight bodies went down into bending position; eight heads curved down.

The starting pistol cracked.

The contestants streaked into the water almost simultaneously in swift racing dives. It was a perfect start, first time.

Leggy, with her length, was already inches ahead.

They came up the first length, Leggy leading the field, Kate Munro a little way behind and the other six bunched together after Kate. In that moment everyone knew that this race was going to be between Ladymount and Hocking.

'She's going to burn herself out!' whispered Tommy in despair. 'She'll have nothing left when Munro comes up to challenge.'

'Don't you believe it,' whispered Sara, but her heart

was thumping. Were Leggy's tactics the right ones? She was already going at a fantastic speed – she must be flat out, surely? While Kate Munro looked as though she had something in reserve.

Leggy turned first with Kate close behind her and now they came down the finishing length, the others dropping farther behind.

'Come on, Kate!' screamed Ladymount.

'Show her, Leggy! Show her!' yelled Hocking School.

The cheers grew louder and louder, swelling into a crescendo. Kate Munro was making her challenge! She was coming up on Leggy, inch by inch! She was level, with only twenty metres to go!

The pool was in uproar. And then an amazing thing happened.

With the sole exception of the Ladymount supporters, whose voices were soon completely drowned, everyone was shouting for Leggy! She was the underdog and the massed crowd was willing her to win! They had taken this odd-looking girl to their hearts.

'L–E–G–G–Y! *Leggy*!' they roared.

They were fighting it out, neck and neck. There wasn't an inch between them. Kate Munro had pulled out everything she possessed but she simply couldn't get past. Leggy was paddling at eight kicks to the stroke cycle and then – unbelievably – she increased the speed of her stroke cycle. Her feet were going so fast in the water that they almost blurred in front of the eye.

She suddenly seemed to leap through the water, as though her body were powered by electricity. Kate Munro couldn't touch her.

She was home!

'LEGGY!' roared the crowd.

The camera flashlights were going, the, the pool was in uproar. Sara and Davy hugged each other, speechless with happiness. Anita Thomas had buried her face in her hands, overcome with emotion.

'She's done it – we've won the Cup!' Then—

'Here is an important announcement,' crackled the loudspeakers. 'Evelyn Legg of Hocking School has equalled the English National Record for the Girls' Junior 100 metres free-style. That is official—'

But the rest of the announcement was drowned in the uproar.

'Evelyn, Evelyn!' Tommy was at the side of the pool, helping the exhausted girl out. 'You've completely bust one minute!'

'I feel as though I've bust my lungs!' choked Leggy.

Sara buried her face in Davy's shoulder, laughing and crying at the same time.

As the spectators clapped and cheered, the other swimmers in the race crowded round Leggy and clapped her on the back, Madge Daltry even hugged her. All except Kate Munro. She turned her back on the others and started to walk away.

'Kate!' exclaimed a tall girl, who was sitting very close to them. It was Joanna Ferguson, who was Captain of Games at Ladymount School. Although only eighteen she had achieved the remarkable honour of playing for the county at both tennis and hockey. 'Aren't you—?'

Kate shook her head vigorously; her face was set and stony.

As Joanna Ferguson left her chair and tried to speak to her, she shook herself free and ran to her changing cubicle. There were tears streaming down her cheeks – the tears of a spoilt child.

'Boooo!' shouted someone in the crowd.

And suddenly there came from all corners the sound of booing and hissing. It subsided just as suddenly as

Joanna Ferguson, head erect, marched straight up to Leggy and shook her by the hand.

'I'd like to congratulate you on behalf of Kate. You swam a wonderful race.'

The crowd cheered, its good humour restored. But Sara and Davy knew that from that moment on Kate Munro would never again be worshipped at Ladymount School.

Then, laughing and exhilarated, they were surging forward with the rest of the supporters from Hocking School: to lift Leggy shoulder-high and carry her once round the pool singing:

'For she's a jolly good fellow.'

When they returned to their seats, Tommy was speaking to Joanna Ferguson and a tall, attractive woman who Sara recognized as Head of Games at Ladymount School.

'We've just been invited to take part in a Swimming Friendly against Ladymount at the end of term, Sara,' said the teacher. She looked very happy. 'I've accepted. That means that as from now we are forming a Girls' Junior Swimming Team at Hocking School, and you shall be its captain.'

'Me!' exclaimed Sara. 'But what about Leggy – I mean Evelyn—'

'Miss Urquhart has also offered our girls the use of their indoor swimming pool for two evenings a week throughout the winter,' Tommy continued. 'I need not tell you that I have accepted her generous offer with the greatest pleasure.'

As the pair from Ladymount School smiled and moved away, Sara said:

'But it doesn't seem right, me being Swimming Captain.'

'Oh, it seems a good choice to me,' said Tommy. She looked at Sara shrewdly. With what appeared to Sara to be quite an extraordinary flash of insight she added: 'You may not be my fastest swimmer, but it has struck me that perhaps you are a good organizer of others.'

Sara went very red.

The pupils from Hocking School sang all the way home. In Leggy's coach, the large silver cup was set high in the back window for all the world to see. Davy and Sara hugged Leggy between them. For a long time there was no need for words and then Leggy, pushing her damp hair away from the back of her neck, said quietly: 'I got my revenge, didn't I? I bet she wishes she never ratted on me to Tommy last Sunday.'

'It wasn't her who rang Tommy,' said Davy. 'It was Sara.'

'*Sara—?*'

'That's right,' said Sara.

'Crikey!' Leggy's eyes grew wider and wider, as the news sank in. '*You* rang her? And you told Davy, and not me.'

'I told Davy on Monday. I had to put him out of his misery. My first plan was to bring everything out in the open by ringing Tommy. But us meeting Kate like that and you thinking it was *her* who'd told on you . . . it was such luck!'

'Why?'

'Because it meant you could work up a really good hate against her of course.'

Sara started laughing, then Davy. Finally, shoulders heaving, Leggy joined in.

'You scheming—!' she cried.

'That's what Tommy said just now. Only not in so many words,' giggled Sara. 'I could be wrong, but I think she's guessed!'

When Leggy climbed out of the coach at Hocking

School, the big silver trophy in her hands, a welcoming party was waiting, for the news had travelled. A figure ran forward, her arms outstretched. It was her twin sister, Vivienne.

'Congratulations. You brilliant thing,' she gasped, and hugged her. 'You're not mad at me are you? I got the time off from school all right, but my lift fell through and there wasn't a single train to Bardsley so I just got a bus straight here.'

Leggy blushed, and Vivienne took it for the old self-consciousness.

But Sara guessed the truth. Not only had Leggy not missed her twin – she had hardly even noticed her absence! She was deeply attached to Vivienne but she no longer depended on her or lived in her shadow. She was emerging as a complete, confident person in her own right now.

'You know, Titch,' said Davy, much later, sitting with Sara in the Take Two coffee bar.

'Know what?'

'Mr and Mrs Legg did a pretty smart thing when they decided to send their daughter to Hocking School.'

'You were the really smart one, Davy. Remember how you said it would do her good to think of something more important than herself for once?'

'Did I?' frowned Davy, trying to remember. 'That was clever of me. Maybe I should be a social worker when I leave school.'

'You'll have to learn how to drink coffee nicely, first,' said Sara solemnly. There was a line of froth all round Davy's lips. 'Right now you look like something out of the Black and White Minstrel Show.'